In Search of Dignity

In Search of Dignity

Rebecca Duvall Scott

26 25 24 23 22   1 2 3 4 5 6 7 8

IN SEARCH OF DIGNITY

Library of Congress Cataloging-in-Publication Data:

Paperback ISBN – 978-10878-8788-3
Hardbound ISBN – 978-10878-7284-1

Published by:
Barefoot Publishing

www.publishbarefoot.com

Printed in the United States of America.

I am bound to them,
though I cannot look into their eyes
or hear their voices.
I honor their history.
I cherish their lives.
I will tell their story.
I will remember them.

~unknown~

In Search of Dignity is dedicated to my parents, Steve & Debbie Duvall, and my uncle and aunt, Mike & Carol Duvall – their lifelong support and encouragement has been invaluable. The Dignity series would not have been a dream come true without their unconditional love.

This book also belongs to my grandmother, Lois Elliott Duvall, and her father, my great-grandfather, John Daniel Elliott, on whose adulthood this story is based. My grandmother told me a few stories about her daddy (who passed when she was only three), and while he was known to carry tales and embellish the truth, we believe he found a sense of joy and peace with his third and final wife, May Wood Elliott Kerr.

Part 1

Leaving Home

1

Johnston Family Farm, Oregon
Summer of 1920

The war that nearly tore this world apart tore me apart instead. It did everyone who was involved, I suppose. But to think that I once was a prosperous farm owner in Oregon, enlisting because it was my honorable civic duty (even if I was sixty-one years old at the time and past my prime) ... if I had known I'd come home a broken man, would I have made the same choices? Would I have stayed home and accepted that growing old was nothing to run from? Would I have admitted to myself that I had nothing to prove? Would life have still found another way to break me? I don't know; it's been two years, and I still can't wrap my mind around it, I thought bitterly.

It's not that I left and things just fell to pieces; that's not the quandary at all. My wife, Clara, did surprisingly well keeping the three-thousand-acre farm running with the help of my foreman, George Walter, our farm hands, and the children who were old enough to help where they could. If my absence left a gaping hole in the functioning of their lives, it slowly filled in while I was away. When I came home, the ground was smooth to walk on and the grass had grown back green and fertile. Therein lies the irritating rub – it was the lingering feeling that they put the puzzle of our lives back together with the extra pieces the war threw at us, and I was discarded as a stray piece. I was staring at a picture I helped create yet was no longer a part of. I guess that's the sad truth of what can be lost when you sacrifice your life for the greater good in any capacity. I still should consider myself lucky. At least I had a life to come back to. Some Great War soldiers never made it home.

I sat in the rocker on the front porch of my large childhood farmhouse, the pride, joy, and wealth passed down to me years ago, contemplating these unsolvable problems while watching my children in the yard. The eight of them had finished their afternoon chores and were playing ball; the older ones gloating their unfair advantage by keeping the ball just out of reach of the younger ones. Charlie tossed it to John over Isa's head, who then stomped her little foot and ran to her big sister, Ella. She swung Isa up and onto her hip in the spitting image of her mother and scolded the boys for always being so contrary.

"If Isa don't like it, she don't have to play with us!" the runt of the litter, Elmer, sneered. The instigating brothers laughed as Isa stuck her tongue out at Elmer. Those two were closest in age and usually close companions, but I had seen him turn on her in more than one scuffle, especially when the betrayal meant possible acceptance by his big brothers!

"Have it your way then," Ella retorted with her nose held high. She put Isa down and took her by the hand. "Next time *you* want something that only *girls* can do – like cooking – you'll eat your words instead!" The boys rolled their eyes as Ella zeroed in on their third sister, Emma. The middle sister had just stolen the ball from John's hands and was undoubtedly hoping not to have to take sides at this opportune moment. "Come *on*, Emma!" Ella hissed.

Emma was the most tomboyish of the girls, but she sure wasn't stupid. Given the ultimatum she would side with her sisters any day. With a sigh, she threw the ball as hard as she could at Charlie and ran to join her sisters. I chuckled as the three of them made a show of stomping off around the side of the house to play by themselves. They were fiery like their mother, and they needed to be. The three of them were outnumbered by five raucous boys.

My sons shrugged and resumed their play, this time keeping the ball from Elmer, who, without Isa, was now the youngest in the game. Elmer scowled deeply, and a laugh escaped me. How fickle life can be sometimes, and oh how that little boy could wail like a girl! He burst into tears and raced around the side of the house in his sisters' wake. He would have to grovel, but I knew tender-hearted Isa would take him back into their fold and hand him a mud pie and little China teacup.

My wife opened the front screen, and I turned at the creaking sound.

"Are you enjoying your afternoon?" Clara asked. Her green dress edged with lace complimented her golden hair, which was braided over one shoulder just the way I liked it. She held out a glass of iced tea with a smile. I took it in my hand and nodded my appreciation.

"It's a nice day – I was just watching the kids play. Do you need help with anything?" I offered, tipping forward in the rocking chair to stand up.

"Oh, mercy, no," she motioned for me to stay sitting and then sat on the arm of my rocker. "The maid is cleaning, and we'll get supper on the table soon. Things run like clockwork around this farm." She winked at me, and I slid my arm around her waist; moments alone were few and far between.

"You and George did a good job of keeping the farm going, Clara. It did a world of good to know he was helping you take care of things when I was away fighting," I assured her for what felt like the millionth time. Other men would probably say I was being too soft by telling her what she wanted to hear, but I was just trying to be empathetic to the fact that the war was rough on both of us.

I drained my tea in a few gulps, liking how it rushed down my throat and cooled my belly. It left me wishing for something a touch stronger, though; sometimes a man preferred to be warm on the inside even on a hot day. I pulled Clara closer, thinking more than a drink could warm a man. Clara kissed the side of my head, like she was doting on a child, and stood up to take my empty glass.

"Well, we couldn't have the man of the house coming home to a mess of a farm, right? I know how hard the war was, honey – you deserve some peace and quiet after all that! I *know* you're still strong and able-bodied, but there are plenty of young men to share in the burden of menial work," she said before firmly changing the subject. "I should call the girls in and start supper. Stay out here as long as you like." I watched as she retreated inside, thinking of how the ten years difference in our age felt like a huge gap these days. When the screen door banged shut, I turned my attention back to the boys.

Clara often claimed she knew how hard the war was, but no one truly understood unless they were in the trenches surviving with us, I thought. I had one good buddy, Elliott, who knew how hard it really had been. He'd carried my bloodied, broken, near-dead body off the battlefield after I had been dragged several feet behind a wagon. If it wasn't for his grit and loyalty, I would've died from that head injury. I couldn't recount that experience to my wife, however;

she was too proper and fragile to hear such ghastly details. That's why I let her continue thinking her words comforted me. It was easier to accept her pity than try to explain the horror of what I had experienced while defending our country.

I shook the harsh memories of war away, stood up, and stretched my body. Another one of Clara's perceptions that needled at me was how, even though I was in my sixties, she knew I still had enough health to work around the farm... yet she had already put me out to pasture in a manner of speaking. *Doesn't she know what a man really needs is to feel useful and respected?* I wondered.

I leaned my shoulder against the nearest porch column, watching the boys scatter to their evening chores before supper; it was calm, quiet, and suffocating without their laughter. With a loud sigh just to hear myself breathe, I walked down the porch steps and headed for the stable. I could at least check the horses' hay and make sure they had water. The summer heat was as hard on them as it was the rest of us.

As I pulled extra hay from a bale and threw it in the troughs, I grew more frustrated. *I am still plenty capable of being the man of this house! I can still work, be a husband, and raise my children,* I affirmed. The longing to feel valuable ate at my insides, as did the desire for my wife to look at me the way she used to. Lots of things changed during the war; as it broke me, it seemed to harden her to love. She barely wanted affection these days, and the children followed her example. Sure, they all hugged me now and again and stopped to talk to me occasionally, like the gentle old pony in the field, but if the kids had a problem or wanted permission to do something they went to their older siblings, the farm hands, their mother, or George... never me. That's what they had become accustomed to when I was gone, and my homecoming did little to shift it back to the rightful hierarchy. I felt like a shell of my former self, an old Great War veteran chewed up in battle, spit out, and just taking up space.

"Pa, Mam says supper's ready," Charlie said, poking his head into the stable. As quickly as he had appeared, he turned and was gone again. I finished distributing the last of the hay bale, allowing him a head start back to the house. My oldest son had no interest in walking back together and making small talk with me... and I had no desire to compel him, at least not tonight.

A maid met me in the foyer with a bowl of water and a rag, and after I washed up for supper, I joined my family in the dining room. My wife and children, four on each side of the table, were standing behind their chairs waiting. I forced a smile and pulled my chair out at the head of the table. Their waiting for me to sit first was a formality I didn't much care for, but again, it was what we were all accustomed to.

The girls sat closest to their mother, who sat opposite me, and the boys filled in the remaining chairs between us. We all quietly ate the beef stew and warm, soft rolls for dipping. Little Isa, forgetting her manners, sucked her broth from her spoon with a slurping noise. With big, surprised eyes, she quickly covered her mouth and looked at her mother in dread.

"I sorry," she whispered. Clara, with pursed lips, nodded for her to continue, and I cleared my throat to try and lighten the mundane mood.

"So," I ventured, hoping to find a way to connect with any one of them, "are you all enjoying your summer?"

"Oh, yes, Pa," they all looked at each other and echoed.

"It's nice to have a break from Mr. Kean," Charlie added, swiping the hair that so often hung in his eyes off to one side. He was looking more like a young man these days, and my heart ached that I didn't know him better.

"I imagine so," I agreed, thinking of the stern tutor hired to come into our home and educate the children. He started with Charlie when he was six years old and had been with us ten years now. He was teaching Charlie down to Elmer, who had just started schooling this year, and Isa would begin next year.

"Children need to cut loose and play hard during the summer, as long as you all are getting your chores done, too," I said, continuing my effort to connect with them. "It takes *all* of us to make this farm go round." I slipped in a hint I hoped my wife would pick up on, too.

"Are you going on your trip to check the fence line this month, Pa?" John piped up suddenly. "I'd sure like to go with you." My heart lifted in pleasant surprise. At the beginning of each month, I took a week to travel to the outskirts of the farm. I usually made the trip with just my horse, Rascal, but I would welcome the time with one of the children!

"John," Clara scolded before I could answer my son. "You *know* your father likes to make that trip alone. It helps clear his head from the bad memories of war – we've talked about that, young man."

I didn't appreciate her speaking for me, but her eyebrows were severely raised. I knew arguing in front of the children would diminish their respect for both of us, so I determined to talk to her in private about the children taking turns joining me on my perimeter checks

– maybe some of the other grievances could be aired, also, if I found the words. I cleared my throat and looked at John. "Another time," I mumbled with a nod. My young son dropped his head and stuffed a piece of bread in his mouth, chewing slowly.

We fell back into eating in silence as dessert was served; if anything, it was just easier. The children dispersed afterward; the older ones staying up a bit longer while the little ones were tucked into their beds by Clara. They each dutifully came to find me in turn and said goodnight, and I kissed the tops of their heads like a loving father should – except for Charlie who had taken to waving at me from the doorway.

The house was quiet when I settled into my office across from the dining room to write some checks for the farm supplies George had ordered. The bookcases full of various works and my father's violin caught my eye instead, and my mind wandered back to simpler times. Father often filled the house with music while Mother read her favorite books. They both seemed content with the life they had built together, and if they had ever been disjointed, I never was the wiser. I wanted that kind of love and home, but if I took a step toward Clara, she took a step back; it was a confusing and exhausting dance wherein we rarely reached each other's arms.

"I'm headed to bed, Daniel," my wife said, her voice pulling me from the reminiscence like a bucket raised from a deep well. Watery thoughts were still dripping over the rim as I tore my eyes from the past and focused them on the present. Clara was leaning against the door facing of the office, arms crossed and head resting on the frame after a long day. Her golden hair was still plaited over one shoulder; she was beautiful.

My chest tightened with desire. Even though we often felt like strangers, part of me still loved a part of her, or at least I loved the woman I remembered her to be. I hoped she felt the same about me. I cleared my throat. "I'll come with you," I said, rising from my desk. "I can finish business in the morning."

She smiled as I followed her up the steps to our bedroom, where she began to undress by pulling her nightgown over her head and slipping her other garments off from underneath. I tried not to stare as I fumbled with my own buttons, even though she *was* my wife and there was nothing shameful in it. She knew I longed for her, but it wasn't very often she let me come close. She always busied herself with chores, reading, or falling asleep before I came to bed... but maybe tonight would be different.

I walked across the room and rested my hands on her hips, pulling her backwards into a gentle hug. She squeezed her shoulders together against my chest and reached back to pat my hip with one hand before turning to face me. I tried to pull her close again, but she ran a hand down the muscles of my arm, holding us apart.

"Not tonight, Daniel, okay?" she said quietly. Her eyes seemed conflicted, and her lips flitted between a slight smile and pouty frown. "I'm just so tired. I guess it's the heat."

With a nod, I shoved my hands into my pockets as she wandered to her side of the bed. I watched her turn down the blankets and climb in, rejection bubbling into anger just under my surface. I tried to bite my tongue. *How does a man even broach the subject of being unhappy in a marriage without upsetting his wife? I want her to understand I mean to work at it – but I need her to want that, too,* I pondered, my breathing quickening.

"Clara, do you still love me?" I asked, spitting the words with more resentment than I intended. The question had eaten at me for so long; it seemed the only place to start. I moved toward her side of the bed and held onto the poster at the footboard to keep a little distance between us. My wife sat up and wrapped her arms around her knees.

"What?" she asked, staring at me. Her face registered shock, then fear.

"Do you *love* me?" I repeated a little louder, digging my nails into the bed post just for the sensation of feeling anchored to something. "It's a simple question."

"Of course, I do, Daniel! Why would you ask me such a thing?" she said incredulously.

I let go of the post and paced back and forth. I had started something and would have to see it through, so I tried to explain – gently – how I felt about life the last few years. Concern filled Clara's eyes until they brimmed with tears.

"So, *you* don't feel like *I* love you anymore... that we don't need you around here. Is that what's been bothering you?" she reiterated slowly after I finished. I nodded, and she gave an exasperated sigh before continuing. "Daniel, the war *changed* you... it changed *all* of us! We're doing the best we can to make it work. These things take time."

"It's been two years, Clara; I don't want to just *make it work* anymore!"

I said too harshly. My wife stiffened and raised her chin defensively, squaring herself for one of our inevitable fights – which is what I had carefully tried to avoid. I chided myself for losing my temper even for just a second; I had lost it on her a few times before and honestly wondered why she had stuck around this long.

"*You* don't want to be with *me* anymore," she incorrectly assumed, her voice trembling. "Is that what you're saying?"

I vehemently shook my head while running my fingers through my hair, trying to calm myself down. "No, *no*, that's not what I mean. I still love you... but this place, this farm... it's grown into something I don't recognize anymore. I need to find *us* again; I need to find a place to fit in. I just don't know how to do that," I replied through gritted teeth.

The honesty surprised us both, and the fight suddenly fizzled into just hurt on both sides. It wasn't my nature to admit I didn't know how to fix something. I needed her to understand my predicament, though. Asking for help to problem-solve was a vulnerable move on my part; I was leaving myself exposed. Clara laid down on her side with her back to me and pulled the sheet up to her neck like a barricade. With my shoulders sagging in defeat, I walked to my side of the bed and sank down onto the edge of the mattress. We were silent for several excruciating minutes.

"I don't know how to help you, Daniel," my wife finally said in a small, shaky voice. "I wish you didn't feel this way. I wish you could be happy here. We worked *so* hard to keep things going so when you came back it wouldn't be another burden for you to bear. We were all so happy that you made it back safely." She paused, choosing her next words carefully because she anticipated the sting. "But it's like you're a shadow of the man I married... and sometimes you can be pretty rough and demeaning. I haven't felt like I've *known* you for a long time now." She wiped at her face, and I knew the tears that ended any argument had come at last.

The stars dotted the darkening sky outside the window as we laid side by side, neither of us knowing how to build a bridge to the other. Eventually Clara's breathing slowed into a rhythm, and I sighed. I tried to roll over and fall asleep, too, but it was no use. *Life was fickle sometimes. That's what I had thought about Elmer's earlier plight as he tried to fit in with his brothers just to have them turn on him. I wasn't much different. I had been trying to fit into life after war – often making a pretty good mess of things – and was also rejected at every attempt. What did Clara expect from me? Could we find a way to rekindle the love we once felt?* I wondered. The questions swirled in my head until sun up, but the answers still evaded me. Of all the things I didn't know, however, one truth rang deep: *I can't go on living like this.*

2

The next morning, Clara and I both pretended the late-night argument never happened. She tended to the children and the house as usual, and I busied myself tying up the month's loose ends with the checkbook. Even without John in tow, I was looking forward to going on the August perimeter check – and *not* because it emptied my mind of bad war memories. The week alone would hopefully clear my head once and for all regarding the way we had been living – and not living.

"Good afternoon, Mr. Johnston," George Walter said as he strolled into my office. My farm foreman was tall and well-built, about twenty years younger than me, and just the sort of able-bodied man I imagined myself to still be. I had considered him a friend before the war, but now we just discussed what we must and otherwise stayed out of each other's way.

"Hey, George," I answered curtly. I motioned for him to come over, and he handed me a piece of paper.

"The farm hands discovered a couple of large, downed trees in the northeastern quarter of the farm. That's the total needed to do the clean-up," he said. "We were lucky it missed the apple orchard by a few feet. I figured you'd want to take care of it soon, though – I know you like to run a tight ship." His flattery fell on deaf ears; we both knew *he* was the one running the ship around here.

I glanced down at the invoice and cleared my throat. "Thanks for staying on top of things, George," I replied. He nodded as I filled out a check, tore it from the book, and handed it to him.

"Have a safe trip this month," George mumbled, walking out of the room.

I watched him round the corner toward the front door before locking my ledgers and financial items back in my desk drawer. Money was one way I could still exercise control in my life; I wasn't about to leave the checkbook laying out for anyone to take my last shred of dignity. As I pushed my desk chair in, I took a moment to lean forward, relieving the sting in my lower back. Sixty-four years of living put a lot of wear and tear on a body, especially when it had been shot at and blown up a few times. I sighed deeply, taking one last glance at my father's violin and all my mother's books on the shelves.

On the morning I was to leave for my week-long perimeter check, Clara came looking for me in the stables. It was just before sunrise; I was almost finished tacking up Rascal by lantern light. It was unusually early for my wife to be awake, and her puffy eyes showed it. She quietly watched me from the doorway as I tightened the girth and double checked my saddle bags. I had already checked my food, water, and tools once, but busying myself kept me from speaking first.

"Daniel," she spoke softly. "Won't you even *look* at me?"

The sun was creeping above the horizon, lighting a fiery hue around Clara's silhouette. I stopped what I was doing to glance up, admiring how her golden hair shone with specks of light, like she had glittering diamonds embedded in her messy morning plait. I cleared my throat and forced my attention back to the saddle. "I don't know what you want me to say," I mumbled, adjusting the stirrups. Rascal whinnied and shook his mane, and I gave him several firm pats for his patience.

"Don't leave angry with me," she pleaded, crossing her arms with a pout.

"*Clara*," I sighed, readying myself to mount. "I'm sorry for all the times I've gotten angry and belligerent with you... but it's not even *anger* anymore. It's more hurt and frustration. I want to keep loving you, keep the life we've built, but I...," my voice trailed off as I gathered my thoughts. "You *barely* let me touch you. The kids hardly know me. George runs everything as well as I ever could. I need a place where I can be the man, Clara." My wife's eyebrows raised as her jaw clenched. I knew I wasn't an easy man to get along with by the state of things; if I was in her shoes, I guess I wouldn't know how to respond to me, either.

I mounted Rascal and steered him toward the door, stopping briefly next to my wife. She tucked a stray curl behind her ear and refused to look up. I knew she was crying again, and I felt the familiar guilt of not being enough to please her. "I've got to head out now, but I *will* be back. Okay? We can talk then," I offered tenderly. She nodded and wiped the tears from her eyes.

"Okay. Be careful, Daniel," she mumbled, turning back toward the house. I held Rascal back, watching her walk up the steps and through the front door, then kicked forward.

The dirt road toward town was lined with trees on each side that graciously offered shade from the rising sun. It was going to be another hot day, but I didn't care. My shoulders relaxed as I put distance between me and the farm. *This week will be simple. I'll travel to the main gate a few miles north of the farmhouse, follow the fence line in a huge square around the property, and head back the same road,* I planned. I could make the trip in about five to six days but always figured in the seventh in case there were several repairs needed. I would take it slow, at a walk, and really try to puzzle things out as I grasped for what was left of my miserable life.

On the first- and second-days' journey, Rascal and I rode mostly in silence. Like most animals, he intuitively understood my state of mind and didn't mind the lack of conversation. There had been five places where the fence had broken down, and I worked diligently during the day to make the needed repairs – my mind and body welcoming the challenge. By nightfall, I made camp and cooked myself supper over a little open fire. When the sun finally melted behind the field, I settled into my bed roll and slept sounder than I had all month. *Once a soldier, always a soldier,* I mused. I was so accustomed to sleeping in the woods on the cold, hard ground, it felt more like home out here in the open than our stuffy bedroom in the farmhouse.

On the third day, with nails sticking out between my lips and a hammer under my arm, I was balancing a railing atop my knee to re-nail it when a surprising thought burst into my mind. I stood up straight to meet it, letting the railing clatter to the ground. *How can I expect Clara to change her ways if I don't? Maybe I have to make more of an effort to take back my authority around home, instead of waiting for them to hand it back to me,* I considered. *Maybe then they would see I was still capable of running the farm and being a husband and father! Maybe I wasn't commanding respect like I did before and during the war, because after the war there was nothing left. I had been waiting for them to tell me I was worthy of respect, like I waited for accolades from my commanding officers.* These novel realizations caused the nails to slip from my lips one by one.

I stood there in the field with my mind ablaze with new possibilities. *If I cut back George's hours around the farm, I could pick up the slack. They'll see me as I used to be before the war. I can prove I'm still a useful asset to this family and command their respect. Clara won't be ashamed of me anymore – if that was even her feeling. I'd work to be kinder, too. She will come back to me, back to a man she feels safe with, a man who can take care of her,* I thought with a smile. I finished mending the fence row and hastily put my tools away. *This was the answer I had been searching for! Why hadn't I thought of it sooner?* Purpose seeped back into my old bones by the minute.

I mounted Rascal and headed in the direction of the farm at a gallop. I had checked three-fifths of the fence, and next month I determined to start out in the opposite direction from the road and check the part I skipped this time. There was an urgency to get home and tell Clara my solution… I would wrap her in my arms, swing her around, and confide in her that I *definitely* wanted to stay married and share this life with her and our children!

The journey took the last hours of daylight, but the farm finally came into view as darkness settled over everything like a warm blanket. The house lights were out and the children in bed when I came through the gate at a trot. I dismounted near the stables and walked Rascal into his stall, untacking him as quickly and quietly as I could. After giving him a bale of fresh hay and water, I decided to leave the saddle bags on the barrel. I would unpack them in the morning.

I was walking toward the house, rehearsing what I wanted to say to Clara under my breath, when a noise halted me in my tracks. There were hushed and hurried voices coming from the barn. It was too late for the farm hands to be working, so I took a few steps toward the sound, hoping nothing serious had happened while I was gone that would require such late-night effort! As I reached for the barn handle to slide back the door, however, I froze like a rifle had been aimed right at me. One of the voices was *Clara's.*

"What is it you expect me to do?" she was saying. "Tell him I want a divorce and marry you instead?"

"Well, why not?" a man answered. The voice registered and my stomach clenched; it was George Walter, my foreman.

"You're beating a dead horse with this discussion; Daniel's the one with the money," Clara hissed back. She sounded exasperated, like they had been arguing for a while now. "This is *his* farm and children, George. I'm *his* wife. My obligation is to him! You've known that's how I felt all along. How would you support me and the kids if we left Daniel, anyway? Where would we go? Our whole lives are here."

"I'd find work on another farm, Clara, and you all could help – at least we'd be together," George muttered.

I gritted my teeth, my hand clenching the barn's door handle. *That no good, dirty, rotten dog of a man was trying to steal my wife!* I thought. My knuckles turned white with hot anger.

Clara laughed skeptically. "You're not thinking this through. All that matters to *you* is loving me, but you're mistaken if you think *I'm* going to slave away on someone else's farm, when I can remain the lady of the house on *this* one," she retorted.

Everything in my vision flashed red as I fully understood the situation. *George wasn't trying to steal my wife*, I realized. *He'd had her for no telling how long, and she was staying with me for the money and security!* I yanked the door open and stormed inside, not needing a lantern to see the rats scurrying to make themselves decent. My foreman and wife had been lying together behind some stacked hay bales, their clothes scattered about.

"Who's there?" Clara asked fearfully, snatching a shawl and wrapping it around her bare shoulders. She squinted out from behind the hay bale and looked horrified when she saw me. She gasped and covered her mouth. "*Daniel?* Daniel – I can explain," she started, scrambling to stand as she fumbled to put her shoes on. "This... this isn't what it..."

"I know *exactly* what this is," I interrupted. Even though my insides were on fire, my voice sounded surprisingly calm. "What I want to know, though, is how long has it been going on?"

George had finally righted himself, too, and he was inching toward me with his hands up defensively. "Now, Daniel – let's just calm...," he said. I punched him before he could finish the asinine sentence, and he fell backward into Clara. She caught him at first, then pushed him aside into the straw to run to me.

"*Daniel!*" she shrieked with pleading eyes. "Daniel, *please*..." she begged. I had threatened her with violence many times before, but this was the first time I almost laid hands on her. I balled my fists instead, turned, and walked out of the barn with her at my heels. "Daniel, just let me explain!"

I wheeled around to face her, and she stopped abruptly, backing up several steps for good reason. "I'll listen to *one* thing, Clara. *How long* has this been going on behind my back?! Weeks? Months? Years? Since I left for war? Before that?" I yelled at the top of my voice, releasing some of my tension. She covered her face and sobbed, dropping to her knees.

"*No!* I was faithful to you for such a long time, Daniel!" she cried. "You must understand what it was like for me! I was alone, running this huge place by myself, trying to care for the kids, worrying if you were alive or dead from day to day... it wasn't until... until you were missing in action that I found comfort with George! I swear it on the Bible!"

I cursed and spit on the ground; the Bible hadn't done me any good all my life, except maybe the day I woke up in the war hospital and learned Elliott had carried me off the battlefield. A priest sat with me day after day, reading scriptures until they swam in and out of my sleep. After I fully awoke, I learned how close to death I had come. It had taken several hours for Elliott and me to be found; I had then slipped in and out of a coma for about two weeks followed by a lengthy recovery. News of our survival trickled back home to our loved ones at a snail's pace... the pieces that had so long felt disjointed fell into place. Sorrow diluted my anger enough for me to see Clara as a fellow victim.

"*He's* why you've barely loved me since I came back," I said, shaking all over. "That's why I haven't felt like I had a place here. You *replaced* me with the next best thing." Resigned to the truth, I turned and started toward the house again. My mind was made up on what had to be done.

"It wasn't like that, Daniel! *Listen to me!*" she begged, hurrying to catch up. "George was able to comfort me when you were away... when I was so scared, and I didn't know..."

I swung around to face her a second time. "And when I got back?" I countered, raising my voice again. I closed my eyes, willing myself to calm down. "I've been home for two years now, and you're still rolling in the hay with another man."

Clara flinched but gathered herself up to full height. "I tried to tell you last night – you haven't always treated me well since you came home, Daniel," she said. "Do you blame me for leaving your bed?"

I spat at the ground again and stalked up the porch steps, through the door, and into my office. Clara caught the screen door before it slammed and woke the children. I had already unlocked my desk drawer and hastily stuffed my important documents and checkbook into a nearby satchel when she rounded the corner.

"What are you doing?" she whispered through her tears. She followed me upstairs to our bedroom, wringing her hands.

I lowered my voice with great effort; I didn't want the kids waking up to this, either. "I'm leaving, Clara," I mumbled, stuffing some clothes and personal belongings into the satchel as well.

"*Please*, Daniel… *please* don't. I'll break it off with George! We can hire a new foreman. I'll be yours again – completely," Clara bargained. Her sobs rose to hysteria in a matter of moments.

"It's a little late for that," I replied, snapping my bag shut and pushing past her onto the second-floor landing. She was right behind me when I spotted Isa and stopped abruptly. Clara bumped into my back on accident but tried to hold on to my shoulders; I shook her off, her touch making me feel ill. My youngest daughter stood by the stairs, looking up at us quizzically; her long, curly hair was all mussed up from her pillow.

"Pa?" Isa said, rubbing her eyes with one tiny fist. "Pa, you come home early?"

"Shhh – yes, honey – I most certainly did," I whispered, glancing back at my guilt-stricken and terrified wife.

"Daniel, *look* at your daughter… you won't leave your children, will you?" Clara whispered in my ear.

My reply was barely audible. "Is she even mine?" I asked. The words were the final blow; my wife took a step back and crossed her arms.

I shook my head in disgust and knelt in front of Isa, softening considerably for the innocent child. Her mouth opened in a wide yawn, and I noticed a few of the other children peeping out of their rooms. I figured the ones I didn't see were listening from their beds, too afraid to come out. Hot tears pricked my eyes for the first time, and I blinked them back. These kids were both the best bits of me to leave behind and the hardest.

"Isa, you listen to your pa now. Your momma made some choices that affected all of us, and I've made choices, too, I guess… it's a mix of both, really, but I can't stay here any longer. I love you and all your brothers and sisters," I said the last part a little louder for all of them to hear. "You all grow up to be good and honest people, you hear?" I choked out.

Isa nodded with her eyebrows knit together in contemplation. "Okay, Pa," she said, reaching to hug my neck. She turned and shuffled back to the girls' bedroom, turning back to look at me for another moment. "Pa, you going back to war?"

I stood up and felt the weight of my bag on my shoulder. "War is preferable to this, sweet child," I muttered. I watched her shrug and slip into the darkness of her room before I headed down the stairs and out to the stables, Clara back on my tail. It was difficult to ignore her pleas and focus on tacking Rascal back up, but I was afraid of what I may do if I faced her again. I had to get away from here and never look back.

I mounted my horse and steered him toward the door, but Clara defiantly stood in the way. When I didn't slow down, she stumbled backward at the last minute with a frustrated wail of anguish. George, who must have hung around for this purpose, ran over and protectively put his hands on her shoulders. He stared up at me as I passed with a look that could kill, but Clara shrugged him off and ran after me. I tightened my thighs around Rascal, and he broke into a canter. Clara fell to her knees crying, and when I glanced back, George was still trying to help her up. I shook my head and bid them both good riddance.

Isa had thought I was going back to war. _I wish there was another war to fight besides this one on the home front!_ I thought bitterly. _In war, at least I fight enemies and not my loved ones._ Clara loving another man and keeping me around for the convenience of money was not a battle I could ever win; I was convinced moving on was the only way we'd all survive.

3

Rascal and I put as many miles as we could between us and the farm that night, each stride distancing me from the problems I'd left behind. When the sun lazily rose in the eastern sky, we were both bone-tired. I eased the horse to a stop at a little hole-in-the-wall saloon near the Oregon – Washington border and tied him to the porch post. Rascal, his chest and shoulders heaving with lather, needed to rest as much as I did. First, however, I intended to drown my sorrows.

I stumbled into the saloon and pushed a wad of cash into the bartender's hand. "I need something strong enough to knock me out... and a room to sleep it off in," I mumbled. "If you can take care of my horse, too, I'd be mighty obliged." The bartender, a large and balding man, took one look at the cash and pushed a whiskey my way with a shrug of his shoulders. I slumped onto a stool, took a long draw, and felt the fire light up my belly. I drained three glasses easily.

They're better off without me, I admitted to myself as misery set in. *Clara can replace me with George, and the kids will grow up with two stable adults to guide them. I was no good at being a husband and father anyway. I'm no good at anything.* No matter what I told myself, the guilt of leaving my family settled deep in my gut. *They're so much better off without me*, I thought insistently.

"You want another?" the bartender barked as my surroundings slid in and out of focus.

I managed a nod but remembered nothing more until I came to my senses in a dank, upstairs room that smelled of urine. Honky-tonk music was blaring below me despite the sun being at high noon outside my window. I rolled over and wrapped the pillow around my pounding head, trying to ignore the smell and once again lose myself in sleep. A knock at the door stirred me fully awake, however, and a small, swimming figure pushed just inside the room. It took my blurry eyes a few moments to focus; it was a young barmaid warily bearing a tray of food.

"You awake today, mister?" she whispered softly, holding the door open with her hip.

My voice was hoarse like I hadn't used it in days. "What do you mean *today*, missy?"

She stood quietly a few moments, biting her lower lip, then answered, "You've been up here for a few days, sir… sometimes I catch you awake long enough to eat a morsel, but you always ask for another drink and pass back out on the bed."

I tried to sit up and the world spun sideways, so I sank my head into my hands instead. "Days?" I questioned through my fingers, swallowing down the acidic bile creeping up my throat. "I… I didn't hurt you, did I?" I had been ornery enough with Clara, and I knew what kind of a monster I was with drink in me.

The barmaid walked into the room and sat the water and plate of mini hard-boiled egg sandwiches on the table, the smell of it nauseating me even more. "No, mister… but I'll be downstairs if you need another drink," she said, slipping out of the room as quietly as she had entered.

I sat still for several more minutes, breathing deeply, then slowly raised my head. The room finally stayed upright, and I noted the urine smell again. Looking down, I saw that the front of my pants was stiff with dried stains. I moaned in disgust before thoughts of my satchel overwhelmed my mind. The possibility of losing my few salvaged belongings spiked my heartbeat, and I glanced around the room frantically. Getting on my hands and knees to check under the bed, I thankfully spied it tucked under the rickety frame close to the wall. Reaching, I grabbed the strap and pulled it out, dumping its contents onto the bed. Throwing the fresh clothes aside, I recovered my important papers and checkbook. Only then did I sigh in relief.

Realizing next how hungry I was, I stuffed the items back into my bag and devoured the sandwiches left by the barmaid; the bread was stale and the egg needed salt, but otherwise it went down okay. It took the rest of the afternoon to wash the stench from my body and clothes, shave, and dress in the only restroom on the floor. Part of the time was spent staring at myself in the mirror; my short, dark hair peppered with gray was just beginning to get shaggy, and my dark eyes were bloodshot and sunken in. At one time I had considered myself fit and ruggedly handsome, but now I hardly recognized my own face. *What kind of a man leaves his wife and children?* the thought crept into my mind before I could shore up my dam against it. I shook my head and wandered back to the dimly lit, dirty room to pack my few belongings. *What's done is done. I must move on,* I reminded myself.

When I walked down the saloon's steps a sober man, satchel in hand, everyone stopped mulling around and looked up with interest. I wondered what gossip had been whispered about the stranger passed out upstairs, but when the bartender cleared his throat, the room's noise resumed full force. He held a whiskey bottle out invitingly. I walked to the bar, shaking my head.

"I'm done with that," I muttered more to myself than him, "but thank you for the hospitality." The bald man raised his eyebrows disbelievingly.

"I've heard that one before," he said with a grin, sliding the whiskey back under the bar.

"I'm one of the few that means it," I replied, swallowing the bitter taste in my mouth. I had wasted days of my life in a drunken stupor; that was not the kind of man I was or had ever wanted to be. Even if I couldn't change things with Clara, I could change things with me. "I've woken up to a new day, and I'll start it with a clean slate," I said. "I'm going to build myself a life I can be proud of."

"Uh-huh," the bartender chuckled with a roll of his eyes. He had probably heard that one, too. "Well, you owe me thirty-five dollars before you start building."

I stuffed my hand in my pocket and pulled out two twenties. "Please give the extra five to that barmaid who tended to me," I told him. Then, thinking of Rascal, I added, "Do you know where my horse is?"

"Down the street to the left – the only stable in town… that's part of the thirty-five," he replied. I nodded and thanked him again, tapping the counter with my fingers in a final goodbye.

As I made my way out the door, down the steps, and into the late evening sun, I determined never to let my shadow darken another saloon again. *This is rock bottom, Daniel Johnston; it's only onward and upward from here*, I told myself. I figured if I kept up the inducement, one day I would believe it.

I retrieved Rascal, saddled up, and together we crossed the Washington state line. It was almost supper time when we stopped in the next town, and, luckily, they had a lawyer's office. *Might as well get business out of the way*, I considered with a shake of my head. When I tied Rascal to the post, however, his ears went back with a shrill whinny. I patted his shoulder and looked him straight in the eye, assuring him I'd be back soon – unlike last time. A few minutes later, I was seated at a table inside the small office with one Mr. Nelson, a tall, thin fellow in a suit and tie.

"What exactly is it I can do for you, sir?" Mr. Nelson asked, drumming his pen on a pad of paper. I had asked him several questions and ascertained he knew the law. Having been in the service, I appreciated doing business with a buttoned up and disciplined man.

I explained what had happened with Clara, figuring he thought me a pitiful businessman in comparison. "My legal matters are pressing," I reiterated. "I want to put my previous life behind me once and for all and be free to move on."

"If there was infidelity on her side, though, you, by law, owe her *nothing*," he stressed.

"I understand," I assured him, leaning forward in my chair with my elbows on the table. I interlaced my fingers. "But she will be raising my children – so, you draft the divorce papers as I've asked and leave her the farm, fully paid, and all my business contacts. There is no need for her to uproot the kids from the only life they've known if it's in my power to make this an easy transition for them." *She'll also be the lady of the house in every meaning of the term*, I thought bitterly to myself. I bit my tongue and slid a check across the table before I could change my mind. "And you give her that check as well. It should keep them afloat until she figures out how to live without my pension." The lawyer glanced at the figure and balked.

"*Five thousand dollars?*" He gasped, nearly choking on the words. He shook his head and adjusted his tie to recompose himself. With one glimpse of my stern face, he bent low over his papers and made the necessary notes, sliding the fully drafted contract and pen back to me to sign. "Where will you go?" he asked. "You'll need to officially change your address so your checks can be forwarded."

"I don't have that detail sorted out yet. I'd like to see all the states in this great country I fought for," I shrugged, picking up the pen. "When I settle, I'll take care of that." I signed the document before sliding a hundred-dollar bill across the table toward Mr. Nelson. "Now, I'd like you to travel to the farm personally, if you will, and handle this with Clara," I added. "Here is a tip to pay your way with plenty left over." His eyes grew large, and he shook my hand before folding the money into his front pocket.

"I'll have this taken care of promptly and discretely, Mr. Johnston," he nodded.

Satisfied, I left the office, grabbed supper at a nearby café, and rented a stall for Rascal at the smithy. Then after my good night's rest in the hotel down the street, Rascal and I headed east. As we wandered down the road, neither of us knowing where we'd end up, I chewed on my thoughts like a hard tack biscuit. Part of my decision to sign over the farm and send the money to Clara was to ensure the care of my children, but I'd be lying if I didn't admit part was for my wife. I was sore upset with her, but the horrors of war had happened to both of us – she was right about that – and the fact that I hadn't been the nicest person to endure as I pulled my mind back together. *Yes, she turned to another man for comfort and accidentally fell in love, her betrayal like a grenade blowing me into pieces. But who is to judge right or wrong but God Almighty himself?* I chewed on that thought longer than the others. *If the tables were turned, I would hope to be faithful until my spouse's return… but you never really know how you're going to handle a situation until you're face-to-face with it. I had been missing in action and gone in general for a very long time. It's no real wonder she made new routines and connections. I came back a different man. She had become a different woman.* It didn't take long for my heart to forgive her, and I hoped one day she and the children could forgive me for leaving them, too.

With no roots to hold me down, Rascal and I traveled through Idaho and into Montana. Weeks passed into months, and as much as I hated to do it, I eventually sold Rascal to a good rancher. My horse needed a home, fresh hay, and a stable to sleep in every night, and I needed a more comfortable riding seat! I could afford any car I wanted, but I chose to buy a Henry Ford Model-T because it was practical for cross-country travel… which I planned to do plenty of.

Passing through Wyoming, I was surprised by the nice roadways. I knew President Harding had sunk thousands of dollars into developing them for better car travel, and with Henry Ford designing a car that the middle-class family could afford, the economy was booming both in the private and public sectors. The farther I traveled and the more I experienced, the deeper I prided myself on being in the thick of such prosperity. It was also a great distraction from having no family or responsibilities, which I thoroughly enjoyed for quite a while.

It took two years after leaving Oregon to finally decide it was time to get out of hotels, and that's when I bought a home in Colorado. I spent most of my time enjoying the local hang outs and events, just floating from one good time to another like a fishing bobber carried by the current. One of the most memorable moments turned out to be the Pikes Peak championship car race that ended in a huge upset. I counted myself lucky to witness Noel Bullock win with his Model-T named *Old Liz* – an unpainted, no hood, tin-can-on-wheels that spectators had nicknamed *Tin Lizzie*. I went back to my own Tin Lizzie that night and patted her on the hood with a chuckle and shake of my head. At least I knew how to pick a winner when it came to cars!

Colorado winters turned out to be too cold for my old bones, though, so I didn't make it six months before selling my house and heading toward California for the sunshine. Railroads had opened the whole country to travel some time before, and it wasn't long until I got an itching to see the eastern United States. I sold my car and traveled by train all the way to Pennsylvania, making frequent stops to wander several states in between. It was truly a spectacular journey… until I met a family boarding in Indiana.

"You traveling alone?" the old man asked me from the next seat over. He and his wife were seated side by side, reminiscent of my parents in their old age, with three accompanying children across from us. I watched the oldest boy, who reminded me of John, read a book while the youngest slept with his head in the big brother's lap. The middle child, a girl, looked out the window with a face full of imagination – like little Isa.

I cleared my throat, feeling the uncomfortable reality of my broken and lonely existence, filled up with stuff and experiences but no meaning. "Yes, I'm alone," I replied, then quickly changed the subject. "Are these your grandchildren?"

The old man smiled and said, "Yes, sir. We've had them for a month's vacation and are seeing them home to their parents. They've been a true delight – we will miss them terribly when we go back to a quiet house with just the two of us."

I watched the children awhile longer, then cleared my throat. "Family is the best thing in a man's life," I said quietly. The old man eyed me knowingly.

"I'm sure you've seen and done lots in your life that can compare," he said. I appreciated his attempt to console a suddenly sullen spirit, but I shook my head.

"*Nothing* will ever compare with having someone to love and being loved," I replied. He and his wife glanced at each other, and the conversation naturally faded as the girl started asking questions about the scenery.

After meeting them and seeing what life could have been like, I became ever more aware that I was living like a boy playing hard outside; I knew night was coming and time was short, so I played harder and tried to ignore that it all would end too soon. For nearly ten years, I had hopped around from town to town – not staying in any one state more than six months at a time. The entire country was my playground, yet here I was still swinging alone. I hadn't made any friends, other than a few fickle acquaintances who liked my money, and as ashamed as I was to admit it, I even spent some time in a mental institution trying to get myself ironed out. One day long after my release, I just woke up and realized how sad my second-chance life had really become. *I had wanted a simple, happy life and the kind of love my parents shared*, I remembered somberly. *So, how is it I managed to build a solitary one after the first attempt failed?* Like that drunk man in the upstairs room of the saloon all those years before, I hated myself. I knew there was nothing to do about it, though, except pull up stakes once again and move on in search of something to fill the infinite void.

One night, a month or so later, when I was between houses, cars, and so-called friends, I sat in a quiet hotel room as the thoughts and feelings flooded my dam. *I've traveled thousands of miles, absentmindedly seeking a love and happiness worth sticking around for… but what if that just wasn't in my cards?* It was a deep, exasperating final thought. I would be seventy-three years old this month; I didn't have much time to keep looking. I wasn't sure anything was even out there for me to find. I considered at that point ending my life – and the misery – but the longing for something real still nagged at me. It was like a persistent fish caught on your line when you're about ready to pack in the pole. I wanted to jerk that sucker and reel it in so my fishing trip wouldn't be a complete bust! *If I could just find one experience that gave me peace again, a joy worth living a little longer for… that would be worth all the time and money I had left,* I concluded. It wasn't in me to give up the search.

I decided to head south toward the Gulf of Mexico the next day; I had been there before and remembered the beauty of where land and ocean caressed one another. Maybe a house on the beach would bring that spark of joy in my last days. I bought my third Tin Lizzie, still my favorite model car, and took a week to travel down through Ohio and into Kentucky. As I pulled into Harlan, a little county near the Kentucky-Tennessee border, I felt the sudden need to stop and rest. I couldn't travel as far and fast as I used to; sitting in the car for too many miles just about killed my hips and back now! I had learned to listen to my body when it needed a stretch, and I was most looking forward to eating some good cooking rather than a gas station's stale chicken or duck sandwich.

I parked my car in front of the town's quaint two-story hotel, grabbed my satchel of belongings from the back seat, and glanced around. I noted the mercantile close by, along with the post office, a few shops, and restaurants stretching down the road, and nodded approvingly. Harlan seemed like a sleepy, little hole-in-the-wall town nestled between two coal mountains – the perfect place to hide from my choices for a while. Little did I know this town held the key to all I had been searching for all this time.

Part 2

Welcome to Harlan

4

It was nearly supper time when I pushed open the door to the Michaels Hotel and was greeted by a pretty, young woman with freckles. She couldn't have been more than twenty-five; her fiery red hair was pulled back in a bun, and she wore the friendliest smile I had seen this side of the Mississippi River. I found her perfect mix of proper yet down-to-earth demeanor instantly refreshing.

"Hello, sir. Welcome to the Michaels Hotel. I'm Carrie – how may I help you?" she asked from behind the tall, wrap-around lobby desk.

"Nice to make your acquaintance, ma'am. I'm Mr. Johnston, Daniel," I offered. "I'd like a room, please… and could you point me in the best direction for supper?"

"Certainly," she nodded, writing my name down before pulling a key from the board behind her. "It's five dollars a night, and you can pay nightly or weekly. We serve a hot supper at six in the hotel dining room over there," she said, pointing behind me at a pair of swinging doors, "and the town's lovely café is across the street and to the left… if you fancy soup and sandwiches."

I nodded with a smile, signed the registry she slid my way, and handed her a five-dollar bill. "I eat plenty of soup and sandwiches while traveling; a home-cooked meal sounds wonderful."

"You travel?" Carrie asked, her interest piqued. She still held my key in her hand, dangling it halfway between the two of us. "It must be amazing to see different places – I've only been down to Tennessee, and that was just one time!"

"Really?" I asked, genuinely surprised and enjoying the small talk. "And why is that?" I hadn't had a real conversation with a woman of any age for a long time. I was also grateful to stand a spell, which helped stretch out my back and legs.

"Well, I grew up here, and this is my parents' hotel. I started working here as soon as I finished school, then I got married and started a family…," she said, shrugging as her voice trailed off. I noticed the ring on her finger for the first time and chided myself for even entertaining the long shot idea that a young gal like her would be interested in an old man like me. "Do you travel a lot because of work?" she asked, suddenly remembering the key. She tucked it into my open palm and crossed her arms.

"That's a long story, my dear," I said, forcing a smile. "If I told you, then you'd be as old as me."

Carrie laughed and shook her head. "Then it best wait for another time! Let me know if you need anything during your stay."

After thanking her, I headed up the stairs to find my room. It was astonishing how neat and clean the little space was, and I realized it had been years since I had stayed anywhere with a woman's touch. I sat my satchel on the bed, and my smile melted away as I lowered myself onto the mattress next to it. With a sudden sigh, I bent over and rested my weary head in my hands. Anytime I stopped long enough to let myself really consider it – a well-off man like myself, able to afford anything I wanted just about, staying in hotels across America with one trusty satchel of belongings – my whole existence struck me as insane. *I should have done so many things differently! No one really knows me. I never stayed in one place long enough to put down a single root. My children don't even know where I am or what has become of me. Who will even come to my funeral when I die?* I wondered, feeling ripped down the middle. Part of me wanted to laugh while the other part wanted to cry. I shook the thoughts from my head and sat up. If I let myself go too deep into the rabbit hole of despair, I'd land myself back in another mental institution for sure – and those places were not friendly. My one life was nearly spent, second chances and all, so I might as well just live out the rest of my days and let the next stranger worry about the rest – including my burial.

I wandered back downstairs to the dining room and was immediately ushered to a table by Carrie. "You do the waitressing, too?" I asked with a grin, my spirits lifting slightly. I had become the master of distracting myself from the weightier topics when needed. She shrugged her shoulders with a smile of her own.

"Yes, and I run the telephone board – when we are short-handed," she answered.

"Well, what do you recommend then?" I asked, tilting the menu for her to glance at, even though I figured she had it memorized.

"Um, the steak and potatoes are probably the best option tonight," she offered honestly, her pen poised above the writing pad. I nodded as she wrote it down and disappeared into the kitchen.

That evening I learned when Carrie Michaels Evan made a recommendation, a man better sit up and listen! The steak and potatoes were the best cooking I'd had in a long time, and the hotel bed she had assigned me was quite comfortable as well. For those two simple reasons, I decided to stay in Harlan a few more days before heading on to the Gulf as planned. In between meals, I leisurely wandered through the shops up and down Main Street – finding a decent tailor to fit me with a new suit was nice, but it was the fishing hole at the edge of town that really captivated my attention. I bought a pole and bait from Corrigans' Mercantile and spent hours catching and throwing back fish from the lake's grassy banks, musing all the time how, in my many travels, I had never stopped in a quaint town like Harlan. The quiet country life was a respite to my frenzied soul.

After about a week of indulgence, I decided to write a letter to my war buddy, Elliott Foster. Out of all the people I had met in my seventy-three years, he was the only one I truly called friend. I had written him from every state I set foot in, but I rarely got return letters because I didn't stay at one address long enough to receive them! That's why I always tried to make a good relationship with the post office employees in each town. If I sent them my forwarding address once I arrived at my new stop – accompanied by a sizable tip – occasionally, I would get a piece of mail from Elliott. His letters were usually forwarded three or four times until they found me but keeping in touch with him was worth my effort. He was the only one who understood my choices and didn't judge all I had done wrong in my life. So, I kept writing – each time thinking maybe I'd stay in town long enough to get a reply.

It was a sunny June afternoon when I walked across the street to the Harlan post office, Elliott's letter in hand. I walked up the steps and pushed open the door before halting my tracks. The most beautiful woman I had ever seen was seated at a desk at the far end of the room, shuffling through envelopes. Her cinnamon brown hair with golden highlights cascaded down her shoulders like leaves in autumn, the front half of it pulled up in an ornate clip – gold latticework with a pink rose in the middle. She was thin but shapely, and her face... it sounded ridiculous to liken her face to an angel's even in my mind, but if I *believed* in angels then hers was how one would surely look! I stood there, just inside the doorway, completely forgetting where I was or what I had come for.

The woman glanced up from her work with a smile that lit up the room. "Hello," she said, rising to walk to the counter. Her long dress nearly brushed the floor, giving the impression that she was floating.

I knew in my bones she was a rare, kind-hearted, and lady-like soul; I searched for the perfect word to describe her... *dignified*. The thought fully formed.

"Can I help you?" she spoke again, her eyebrows knitting together with a lovely hint of concern. "Sir, are you okay?"

"Yes, *yes*," I stammered, closing my eyes for a moment. Not many experiences made my childhood stutter emerge. I couldn't think straight when looking at her! I couldn't remember ever having a feeling like it, not even with Clara. "I... I want to mail this letter please," I said, opening my eyes. Any embarrassment melted away to see her warm smile again. I held Elliott's letter out, my hand slightly trembling, and she took it. Her fingers softly brushed against my rough knuckles, and the sensation lingered.

"I can do that for you," she said, nodding with a wink as she turned back to her desk.

Does a woman's wink mean the same thing as a man's? I pondered, watching her shuffle through some envelopes. She slipped Elliott's letter in between two of them, then glanced back over her shoulder.

"If I may ask, are you Mr. Johnston?" she continued. I was surprised she knew my name but then remembered it had been on the envelope.

"Yes, ma'am," I replied. "You can read my chicken-scratch writing?" She laughed. It was a lofty, soft-around-the-edges sound. I immediately wanted to hear it again.

"I've seen worse handwriting, believe me... I used to be a teacher. But no, I ask because Carrie told me there was a gentleman traveler staying at the hotel. Harlan doesn't get a lot of traffic, so new faces are easy to spot," she explained.

I smiled, stuffing my hands deep in my pockets. "The Michaels family has been quite accommodating. Their hotel is very comfortable – soft bed and good food – that's actually why I stuck around this last week."

The woman wandered back toward me and crossed her arms. "They're good people," she agreed. "Carrie's my best friend."

"Really?" I asked, glancing down at her hands. She didn't wear a wedding ring. "That letter there is to *my* best friend. We served in the war together."

Her eyebrows lifted along with the corners of her mouth. "It's not every day I get to meet a veteran – I sincerely thank you for your service, sir!"

I was used to being hollowly patronized as a serviceman, but I could tell she really felt gratitude. "You're welcome," I answered just as earnestly.

After a few moments of silence, she motioned to her desk with several stacks of mail atop. "Well, I better get back to work," she said, rolling her eyes. "They won't sort themselves, sadly."

"You work here?" I asked. The words slipped out before I could think how idiotic they sounded. She was behind the counter in a post office for heaven's sake! I looked at the floor, and when I looked up again, she was smirking. I laughed and shrugged my shoulders. "Silly question, huh?"

"Well, yes and no. I'm in town visiting Carrie for a while and just filling in for Mr. Murphy here at the post office. He's had some health issues lately... I happened to be in the right place at the right time is all," she replied. I could second that twist of fate.

"It's nice when things work out like that," I affirmed. She looked back at her desk, and I took the subtle hint. "Well, maybe I'll see you around." I forced myself back toward the door, feeling like a foolish schoolboy gawking at a girl I could never have. It was not lost upon me, either, that it had been a *long* time since any feeling like this had been stoked. I had actually thought my self too old for attraction.

"Sure – I'll be here," she smiled, adding, "for a few more weeks at least."

"Me, too," I said, deciding instantly to stay as long as this beauty did. I reached for the doorknob. "It was really nice to meet you."

When I pushed out into the sunshine, I came down the post office steps with a skip in my stride. *What a beautiful day!* I mused as if seeing my surroundings for the first time. I let my mind wander to an impossible yet extraordinary possibility. *Could a gorgeous young woman like her ever fall for an old codger like me?* I chuckled at how scattered she had made me feel, and then realized – I hadn't even asked the angel's name!

5

nna Beth Atwood was her name... I asked Carrie when I got back to the hotel that evening. Carrie liked to talk, and I gleaned as much information about the gentle, pretty Miss Atwood as I could! For some reason beyond my rational understanding, that young woman in the post office had never married, and she quickly became the only thing I deemed worth pursuing in the twilight of my life. It was like an invisible thread had been tied between us as we stood there chatting over mail, and now that connection was tugging at me incessantly. I couldn't explain it, but this woman was important.

Carrie and Miss Atwood had been best friends since Miss Atwood moved to Harlan at twelve years old. Even though she only stayed in town for a couple of years, she and Carrie had kept in touch – much like Elliott and me. Miss Atwood moved to Tennessee before her fifteenth birthday with her mother, grandfather, and little sister, and after finishing her education at Wesleyan Women's College in Georgia, she had taught in a one-room schoolhouse in North Carolina for two years.

"The economic depression was hard enough," Carrie had told me during our chat, "but last year, her grandfather passed away. He was such a good man... Anna Beth loved him with all her heart." She paused, lost in a memory I didn't want to disturb. Her face was also fluctuating between emotions I couldn't quite decipher, but she finally shrugged her shoulders and continued. "Anna Beth ended up coming back to Harlan with me after the funeral. Her grandfather is buried at the church... and

I think she had unfinished business to take care of here." I nodded and thought it best to stop asking questions. I didn't want Carrie thinking my keen interest was anything more than polite conversation.

I took to visiting the post office daily after that, however. The sight of Anna Beth Atwood was like setting a spark to ash that had burned out and gone cold. The warming sensation of feeling alive again was addictive. I said I was just checking for return letters from Elliott, even though I knew it would take at least a month for my most recent letter to reach him and for his to travel back. I further explained how I always left word at previous towns to have my mail forwarded to my next location, so I was *also* watching for older letters to find their way to Harlan. Miss Atwood didn't seem to mind my stopping by, anyway; in fact, she acted as if my idle chit chat and occasional story were genuinely interesting! This, too, meant a great deal to me. In the past ten years of travel, not one person had paid me any mind unless they figured money as a reward for the effort.

Back in the quiet hotel room at night, however, fears would douse the tender yearning to feel connected to someone once again. Like an alcoholic coming out of his dazed stupor, once alone I would crash back down to reality. *Why am I staying in this little, podunk town, visiting a woman nearly a third my age every day? It's crazy!* I chided myself – maybe I was really and truly addled. *There is a lifetime between us. I'm nearing the end of mine, and hers is just really beginning. There was no way she'd ever need or want me the way I desired her... she still had years to make those kinds of meaningful relationships.* By the time I fell asleep at night, I had resigned myself to the fact that this foolish behavior of mine had to stop. Then each morning I'd wake with an undaunted sense of adventure and hope in my breast! The mere chance of seeing her one more time was enough to get me up and moving again.

After about two weeks of regularly checking for mail just so I could seize a few moments with Miss Atwood, I paused at the post office door with my fingers wrapped around the knob. I was working and reworking what I could say to gain more than just a few minutes of small talk; I wanted to go and sit somewhere, just the two of us, and listen to *her* talk for hours. I wanted to be lost in the beauty of who she is, who she was, and whoever she wanted to be. *But how does an old man ask a young woman on a date?* I pondered. *Do seventy-three-year-olds even go on dates?* I chuckled at the thought. *I am insane. I'm playing the part of a fool in some romantic comedy!*

"Hello, Mr. Johnston," that sweet voice from my dreams said from behind me, startling me back to the present.

I turned around to see Miss Atwood smirking up at me from the base of the post office steps. I took my hand from the doorknob and plunged it into my pocket, confused. "Well, hello, Miss Atwood! You're not working today?" I asked, glancing back at the post office. I hadn't seen her outside its walls until now.

She shook her head and tucked a strand of golden-brown hair behind her ear. "No – Mr. Murphy is well now. He doesn't need me anymore," she replied.

I let that soak in, my smile faltering. She would have reason to leave Harlan now, and the thought of not knowing where she'd travel on to incited panic in my chest. I reminded myself this was the most foolish of endeavors – a star-crossed love interest doomed from the start – and I shouldn't get worked up about it fatefully coming to an end. I walked down the steps, trying to decide if it would still be better to ask and be rejected than to live the rest of my years wondering *what if.* I swallowed. "Well," I ventured bravely, my heart pounding in my throat, "would you like to accompany an old man to lunch then? I'm buying."

Miss Atwood crossed her arms, considering me with kind, yet guarded, eyes. Then she smiled. "I would like a bite of lunch, Mr. Johnston, but I pay my own way," she said, accepting with a caveat. My heart skipped a beat as it settled back into my chest, and we set off down the street to the café side by side.

I held the door open and took in her looks as she walked past me. Her white blouse had lace on the collar and cuffs, and it was tucked in neatly to her blue, ankle-length skirt. She carried herself with an attractive mix of pride and humility, and I could smell a dash of perfume. The wonderful mystery of this woman flooded my imagination again; I wanted to soak in every detail.

The café was packed, but we spotted a small table by the window and weaved our way toward it. I pulled out her chair, and she nodded her appreciation. The waitress hurried over to take our order, and after bringing us our drinks, I glanced around – suddenly self-conscious. *Was Miss Atwood embarrassed to be seen out with someone my age? She surely preferred younger company*, I worried, my heart sinking a little. *This lunch was just a gesture of kindness on her part to save my feelings.* I looked across the table at her uncertainly, and she smiled that warm angel smile of hers. If she was embarrassed at all, she hid it well. I cleared my throat and smiled back.

"So, how often did you and Carrie write each other as children?" I asked. Our mutual devotion to letter-writing was the only conversation starter I could think of.

"Weekly, if we could," Miss Atwood answered, taking a sip of her strawberry lemonade. Her delicate lips curved around the glass's edge and left a ring of light-colored lipstick on the glass. "How about you and your friend, Elliott?"

I swallowed a swig of my sweet tea. "I try to write whenever I stay in one place for a week or more, and I'm sure he writes me when he can, too," I answered. "I've only received a few of his return letters over the last ten years, though. I imagine there are a lot more floating around the states looking for me... I just move around too much to be found."

Miss Atwood studied me, and I found it appealing how she didn't rush to fill the empty space in our conversation. "You know, you've never really told me *why* you travel so much," she finally pointed out. I took the invitation to move the conversation to a deeper plane.

"To be quite honest, I came home from the war a different man. War was equally hard on my wife and our children, and she took comfort with my farm's foreman. I can't quite blame her. I was pretty mean and difficult for a while – trying to sort it all out and pull my life back together didn't go well. I chose to leave them rather than work at it, and I've been a traveling man ever since," I said, laying out the ugliest part of my life first thing.

Miss Atwood just nodded compassionately. If she thought ill of me for what I had done, she didn't show it. Our gaze briefly tangled in the silence, then broke as the waitress brought our soup and sandwiches. I watched Miss Atwood take a bite of her turkey sandwich and wash it down with another sip of lemonade. "Where all have you traveled?" she asked, dabbing at her mouth with the white linen napkin.

I picked my sandwich up and dipped it in my soup. "I've seen every state in the union and have had a residence in half of them," I said.

Miss Atwood nearly choked on her second bite but recovered quickly with a cough. "You're kidding now," she laughed skeptically, holding her napkin over her mouth.

I swallowed my sodden bite and shook my head. "No, ma'am. That's the truth," I replied.

"*Wow,*" she exclaimed. "That must have been amazing! I was born in Missouri and have some family left there, but my parents brought me and my younger sisters to Kentucky when I was twelve. I lived in a foster home here in Harlan for almost three years, then moved to Tennessee with my new family... then college in Georgia, and teaching in North Carolina," she offered, counting the states on one hand while she spoke. "That's only five states! I can't believe you've been to all forty-eight!" Carrie hadn't told me her friend had been in a foster home, and while I wanted to know more, I decided now was not the time to ask. Those situations are often tender subjects, and I did not want to ruin the mood.

I shrugged my shoulders; visiting forty-eight states was no big deal to me. Miss Atwood laughed again, and lunch continued to be enjoyable. When we finished eating, I paid my bill and watched her pay her own as she was insistent, and then I asked if I could walk her home.

"Where are you staying?" I asked, holding the café door open for her. "I know you're visiting Carrie, but I haven't seen you frequent the hotel."

"Carrie's parents live in the back of the hotel, but she doesn't. She and her family own her parents' old house down in the valley past the church. Carrie just comes to work early and leaves late – and she brings the kids to play in her parents' apartment or out in the town. That's probably why you figured they all lived in the hotel," Miss Atwood explained. "I'm staying with Carrie – but at her house, not the hotel."

I nodded. "Well, I would fancy a walk through town; it's good for the old bones, you know," I said with a wink. I hoped by joking about my age, the fact that I was nearly triple hers wouldn't matter as much.

"I would fancy the company, then," she said with a wink, "and for the record – I don't think you're *that* old."

I laughed at her kindness as we wandered past the little fishing hole, down the hill, and out of town in a direction I hadn't ventured yet. She pointed out the schoolhouse, where she attended classes with Carrie for the two-and-a-half years she was in Harlan, then a way further she pointed out a charming, little white church nestled atop a sloping hill.

"And *that* is where the Lord saved my soul," she said matter-of-factly. I gathered it was a significant memory of hers and nodded, although I wasn't sure what she meant by *saved*.

"It's a beautiful church," I said dutifully.

"Do you go to church?" she asked. No one had ever asked about my faith before, and I just shrugged my shoulders.

"Well... I don't *not* go to church, if you know what I mean," I replied. "I guess I would consider myself of the Christian Scientist faith if anything. I like to learn about all sides and make my own decisions rather than having a church tell me what to believe in." Miss Atwood considered my answer carefully for a few moments, and we walked on in silence.

"I used to go to church all the time with my family in Missouri," she finally picked the conversation back up. "I was lucky this one in Harlan believed the same way, and then we found another back home in Tennessee, too. When I was teaching in North Carolina, however, I was so busy and overwhelmed by life that my faith was neglected. I really struggled with keeping hold of it and moving forward, you know? Once I got straightened back out, I determined to go to church every time the doors are open. My grandfather always said if I built my life around God, He would add everything I needed to it."

"Carrie told me you were close to your grandfather," I mentioned. She nodded.

"Yes, very. He was one of the most important people in my whole life. He got away from his faith at one time, too, so I really trusted him to lead me right," she confided.

It was my turn to be quiet while I mulled over this deep conviction of hers. I had never really found anything faith-wise worth building my life around, nothing that I wandered from or ever felt the need to come back to. Secretly, I wondered if there even was a God out there who would want me after the life I had led. "I think church and believing in God is a mighty fine thing," I offered, nodding sincerely. I decided at that moment if faith meant that much to her then there must be something I had missed along the way. A second thought whispered in my heart, *Maybe it's not too late to still find it.*

Miss Atwood smiled and, surprisingly, took hold of my hand. As we walked on, she gave it a little squeeze, and a warmth spread through me like electricity. Then, just as unexpectedly, she let go and ran her hand over her hair, her cheeks flushing slightly.

After clearing her throat, she said quietly, "You're one of the most interesting men I think I've ever met. In some ways you remind me of my grandfather, Mr. Jingle, but also like a man I met in North Carolina – but so much wiser." I grimaced to be compared to her grandfather but then remembered he had been one of her favorite people. I also wondered who in her past had been unwise enough to mess up a chance of winning her affection.

"Well, thank you. I think you're wonderful, too… and you called your grandfather Mr. Jingle?" I wondered aloud. Miss Atwood laughed.

"That part of my life is an interesting one," she countered, and I figured she was speaking of her time in foster care again. *There's that mystery I want to unravel*, I thought to myself.

"I'd love to hear about it if you care to share," I fished.

As we walked further into the valley, farming land stretched out as far as I could see with fields of yellow-topped corn, potatoes, beans, and tobacco. Miss Atwood crossed her arms and told me how her parents came to Harlan in hopes of building a better life in coal country. I was shocked to hear, however, that by the time they arrived, they had lost just about everything.

"They parceled me and my sisters out to different neighbors and intended to come back and get us," she continued, "but they never did." With every step, Miss Atwood began to look more like the lost girl she spoke of than the grown woman I knew her to be. She shrugged her shoulders with a notable exhale. "We *still* don't know what happened to them. One of my sisters ran away back to my oldest sister in Missouri, another we just recently tracked down, and as far as me and my baby sister, Olivia, our foster mother, Grace, took us in permanently. The three of us moved to Tennessee with Mr. Jingle and started a new life together."

We walked a few paces in silence. I didn't want to pry any further as I knew this conversation was dredging up a lot of emotional sediment, but I didn't want to seem insensitive, either. I was just about to offer my apologies when her arms relaxed back down to her sides.

"Mr. Jingle was a *Godsend* in my life," she said, rebounding in her emotions. "If I had known my real grandparents, I would have hoped they would have been like him." *A Godsend*, I thought. I found her choice of words uncanny. *That was the perfect word to describe my feelings for her.*

"So, how do I remind you of him?" I asked, finally finding my voice again. "Is it the old part?" I slipped in the joke with a chuckle, attempting to lighten the suddenly heavy mood.

Miss Atwood glanced at me and giggled. "You'll be pleased to know that age has *nothing* to do with it, Mr. Johnston," she said dismissively with a wave of her hand. "You remind me of him because you are kind and full of stories… and mostly, I think, because you're a wanderer. Mr. Jingle lost his family in a house fire, which I know is different than how you lost yours, but it made him buy a truck and travel the countryside, also – just to stay away from the memories.

"He settled down again after taking Grace, Olivia, and me in, of course – and if it wasn't for his help and guidance, I don't know how we would have made it on our own. Mr. Jingle was a peddler of sorts in addition to a preacher. He opened a store in Tennessee, and Grace sells her handiwork there. We didn't have a lot, but we had enough… and we had all the joy, laughter, and love our hearts could hold. We were happy, and I learned that's what matters most."

Miss Atwood looked away toward a field of corn, and I marveled at her understanding of life's weightier matters. *She calls me wise? Not only was she beautiful, interesting, and able to make me feel alive again, she understood how a simple life full of joy and love was the most precious gift of all!* I also thought of how her grandfather had his share of heartache with losing his family in a fire but settled from a transient lifestyle after taking Miss Atwood and the others in. I hadn't felt settled in a very long time. The last couple of weeks in Harlan – with her – was the most settled I had felt since before the war, I guessed. I was beginning to think Miss Atwood just had a settling effect on men in general.

When we came to a fork in the road, I realized my companion was lost in her thoughts, too. She was staring down the right road, which dipped further into the valley, while the left fork arched up another hill. Her face was ashen, like she had seen a ghost down that lane.

"Miss Atwood, are you alright? Is that the way to Carrie's house?" I asked her, concerned. She only just glanced at me before recomposing herself, but it was long enough for me to see that sadness had darkened her bright eyes.

"No," she replied quietly, shaking her head while running her hands over her hair again. She pulled her golden-brown waves over one shoulder and tightly held the locks in her fist. "That's the way to the Graingers' farm, where I lived in foster care for almost three years." She cleared her throat and motioned to the left road. "Carrie's house is just a bit further up this hill."

I followed her silently, wondering if something terrible had happened at the Graingers' farm or if she just still missed her biological family. It was another thing I didn't want to ask, however, and it wasn't long before we came upon a nice house with a white picket fence. She stopped at the gate with a shrug of her shoulders, releasing her hair and shaking it loose again.

"This is where I'm staying," Miss Atwood said, forcing a smile. "I'd invite you in for tea, but no one else is home yet; I wouldn't want to be improper."

I nodded, liking that she had so much virtue. "No, you're much too dignified for that," I said with a wink. "I would expect nothing less!"

Her eyes grew wide, and I immediately worried I had said something to offend her. Next thing I knew, though, a genuine smile was spreading across her face again.

"What did I say?" I asked with a laugh. I was following her emotions up and down like an ocean-side pier carnival ride. I had ridden one of those about nine years before, and here I was clinking up the incline again with anticipation of the dip that always catches the stomach.

Miss Atwood put her hands on her hips and sighed deeply. *"Well...* I can't hardly believe it, but Mr. Jingle nicknamed me Dignity when I was a girl. It meant a great deal to me – helped define me even – and you just called me *dignified*. It's such an uncanny coincidence."

I nodded in agreement. "I can certainly see why he thought it a fitting nickname," I said, wishing now more than ever that I had known this Mr. Jingle, too.

"Thank you kindly for today, Mr. Johnston," Miss Atwood replied, pushing through the gate at last. She fiddled in her purse and pulled out a house key on a small ring. "I've appreciated your company and you taking time to walk me home. Can you find your way back to town?"

"Yes, ma'am, it's a straight enough shot back up the road and around the bend," I assured her.

We bid each other goodbye as she walked toward the house, turning before the porch steps to wave another farewell. I waved back and waited until she was safely in the house before starting back to town, whistling a lively tune as I walked. It would be a lie to say there wasn't a new spring in my step, and I didn't even care if it was short-lived! For now, at this very moment, I felt life was once again worth the living.

6

Later that week, I learned Carrie had invited her friend to stay in Harlan until she found another teaching job, and Miss Atwood took her up on the courtesy. She took to looking in the newspaper every day for school position openings in the surrounding areas. If God heard the supplications of a Christian Scientist, I hoped the continued economic downturn we had been having would stretch out her search! I would stay as long as she stayed, and when she moved on, I guessed I would head to the coast as previously planned. I told myself I just wanted to make sure she got on her feet again, so I wouldn't always wonder what had happened to her, but really, I knew I was hanging around to see if she'd ever return my interest.

"So, why did you become a teacher?" I asked Miss Atwood one warm afternoon. I was leaning back on my elbow on a picnic blanket spread out by the lake, and she was sitting next to me, eating a peach while watching the occasional fish jump. We had enjoyed several lunch dates after the first, but this was our initial early evening outing. I watched her curiously, still trying to furtively explore what made her tick. She was unlike anyone I had ever met before, and that fascinated me to no end.

Miss Atwood swallowed her last bite, dug a little hole in the dirt next to her, and buried the peach pit. She winked at me, like growing a peach tree from a seed right there by the lake would be our little secret. "Well, I wasn't supposed to advance past the seventh grade," she confided. "If my family had stayed in Missouri, my momma would have brought me home to work around the house and tend to my younger sisters. When we came to Harlan, however, Grace let me continue my education... even after we moved to Tennessee. She encouraged me to go on to college, too. I wanted to be a teacher because I'm thankful for my own educational opportunities... I wanted to help other children like me succeed in school against all odds."

"Very noble and *dignified*," I said with a grin. She blushed and flashed me her angelic smile, which is what I was after.

"If you want to know the whole truth," she said with a smirk of her own, "I *also* had a judgmental teacher while I was here in Harlan – Mrs. Sensley. She didn't treat me fairly, so I guess deep down part of me wanted to become a teacher so I could advocate for my students in a way I felt others failed me." She paused, a torn expression on her face. "Now, how dignified is that, Mr. Johnston – to become a teacher just to right the wrong done to me?"

"*Still* the definition of dignity in my book," I answered confidently. "I bet you helped a lot of kids while you were in North Carolina." She shrugged humbly.

"I tried," she mumbled. After another pause, she glanced at me out the corner of her eye. "Enough about me. Did *you* always want to be a soldier?"

"Heavens, no," I replied, shaking my head quickly. "I only enlisted because it was my civic duty. I figured I would get called up eventually, so better get it over with on my terms."

"What did you want to do with your life then – if not be a soldier?" Miss Atwood asked, shifting positions. She adjusted her long, flowing skirt over her legs, and wrapped her arms around her knees. I appreciated her modesty as much as her intrinsic beauty. After the moral decline of the nineteen-twenties, there weren't a lot of women like her left in the world and I suspected it would only get worse.

I cleared my throat, bringing my thoughts back to the conversation. "I wanted to be like my father and run the family farm. My ex-wife and I lived in my childhood home on three thousand acres. I was living my dream... until it wasn't my dream anymore," I said, picking a little yellow flower from the banks and twirling it between my fingers by the stem.

"*Three thousand acres?!*" she exclaimed. I nodded and offered her the flower. She took it with a sheepish grin and stuck it behind her ear. Yellow looked good in her cinnamon-colored hair.

"Does that make a difference in how you see me?" I asked quietly. She didn't seem to care that I was considerably older than her, but I wondered what she'd think about my financial stability despite being an immoral wanderer. We hadn't broached that topic yet, and I was always waiting for her to realize how ridiculous spending time with me was.

Miss Atwood firmly shook her head. "No, sir. I figured you came from an affluent background given you've seen every state in the union and owned a house in half of them!" she surmised. "But three thousand acres... that did surprise me. You're quite humble for having such a good start in life." She paused, looking out at the lake for a moment. "Do you miss your first family, though?" she asked quietly.

I dropped my head as sadness stirred within me. I didn't like discussing what felt like a lifetime ago, even though I *did* think especially of mine and Clara's children daily. "I miss what we should have been, if that makes sense," I confided. "Part of me still loves the Clara I remember – before the war – but it's like she died along with that old version of myself. I still deeply love my kids, too, but I truly feel they are better off without me." Miss Atwood took the flower from behind her ear and twirled it between her fingers for a few minutes. My anxiety mounted the longer she stayed lost in thought.

"I completely understand why you left Oregon, Mr. Johnston," she finally spoke, "but what I wonder is if your children understand. You know how my parents brought us to Harlan, left us in foster care, and never came back... truth be told, I obsess about the reasoning even today." She paused to inhale slowly; I could tell she was weighing her words carefully. "All I'm saying is that at some point in your life, you may want to reach back out to them."

The tightness in my chest relaxed. She wasn't judging me for my past; she was trying to help me. "Tell me more about your family," I requested, steering the conversation back toward her. Miss Atwood grinned, knowing exactly what I was doing.

"Well, my baby sister, Olivia, got to stay with me at the Graingers. We are birthday sisters – we share the same birthday but ten years apart – and we've always been close. She's now fifteen and just a *beautiful* soul," she offered.

I listened to Miss Atwood talk about the sister she helped raise and saw a deep love stirring in her eyes. I also did some quick math; if the two women were ten years a part... that made Miss Atwood twenty-five years old. I rubbed my chin and swallowed my nagging concern. *Fifty years* difference between us! It suddenly felt like an insurmountable odd when you put a number on it, like a delicate bubble of possibility popping just out of reach.

"When I was fifteen, I was having the worst time of my life," she continued. "But Olivia got to grow up so differently than me. There's nothing damaged about her... she's planning on going to college to be a nurse, and she'll be great at it. She's got a heart of gold – a servant's heart – just like Grace."

Damaged. The description of herself caught me off-guard. I had never thought of Miss Atwood as anything but perfectly whole. I wanted to better understand her insecurities but was still afraid to meddle. "Didn't you say you had other sisters?" I asked a safer question, and she nodded.

"My oldest sister, Martha, didn't come with us to Kentucky. She had only been married to her husband, Jonathan, for six months when we left," she explained. "They've had several children of their own now, and my younger sister, Janie, was the one I told you ran away. She was only nine years old at the time but somehow made it all those miles back to Martha in Missouri!" I raised my eyebrows in surprise, and Miss Atwood laughed with an appreciative nod. "Yes, I know – it was over *five hundred miles* on foot."

"I'm glad she made it safely," I replied, shaking my head in disbelief. "Is that all of your sisters?"

"No, I had one more – Emily. She was a year younger than Janie and placed in yet a different home. Her foster family moved to another town shortly after they took her in, and we completely lost track of her. It wasn't until the year before last, when she was able to track down Martha's address through the Corrigans' Mercantile, that we all reconnected. She's twenty-one now, just married, and pregnant with her first child. She actually married the son of her foster parents," she said.

I nodded with a chuckle; this woman had an amazing story! "I guess it was nice to raise their daughter-in-law, huh?" I joked.

Miss Atwood shrugged her shoulders and smiled slightly. "I guess so. They're all happy at least... that's what matters," she said. I noted the lilt of sadness in her voice and cleared my throat, sorry to have made light of a situation that had obviously devastated most of her young life.

"And no one has heard from your parents in all this time, not even the oldest daughter who stayed behind?" I inquired seriously. The parents' disappearance was the piece of the mystery that just refused to unravel. *What kind of parent would leave their children to be raised by strangers? What could have happened to them that they couldn't come back as promised?* I wondered.

Miss Atwood shook her head, looking out at the lake for a long moment. "I received one letter early on that said they were still looking for a job so they could get a house and bring us home by Christmas, but that was it," she confided with a sigh.

Without thinking, I reached across the blanket and laid my hand on hers. "I'm so sorry, Miss Atwood," I said earnestly. When she didn't move her hand out from under mine, our eyes connected. I once again felt that familiar spark of wonder and desire add kindling to an ever-growing fire within.

"I appreciate your sympathy, Mr. Johnston, but it was a long time ago," she said. "And please call me Anna Beth." I smiled as we notably moved from a formal to more personal level. This was a step in the right direction!

"Well, Anna Beth, it may have been a long time ago, but our experiences shape our whole world. They influence how we see everything around us," I replied.

"They do indeed," she agreed with a nod, a gentle smile tugging at the corners of her mouth. "But we *don't* have to let the memories consume us."

We visited with one another every day for a month after that evening at the lake. Most of the time she accompanied me to a meal or on a walk, and it was no surprise when we started to get strange looks from people who had seen us together repeatedly. *The seventy-five-year-old man with the twenty-five-year-old girl,* I knew they were thinking, *how unseemly.* If Anna Beth noticed the judgmental stares, she never let on. That was one of the many, small reasons I cherished her more with each passing day.

There was one problem, though; I didn't know if she shared my feelings at all. *What girl her age and in her right mind would want to be with the likes of me?* I reasoned. I kept trying to think of a way to tell her how I felt, but finding the right words was like grasping for straws. That's why one day I waited for her outside the hotel, bit the bullet, and just invited her to a picture show and supper – come what may. Carrie had mentioned the theater on the edge of town had just recently been built. Perhaps a more romantic gesture, with the added magic of movies and a starlit stroll, could muster in me the courage I needed to expose this old heart of mine one more time.

"A picture show?" Anna Beth questioned, pausing on her way to the dress shop. Her smile instantly put me at ease; I knew she'd say yes. "I've never been to one!" she breathed excitedly. Her wavy hair fell over her shoulders, and the blonde hues mixed into the light brown glinted like specks of gold in the afternoon sunshine.

"Well, then, we must go! How about tonight – and supper after? Seven o'clock? We can dress up and make a night of it," I offered. She nodded without hesitation.

"It's a date, Mr. Johnston!" she confirmed with a grin, strolling off in the direction of the dress shop as she waved goodbye. "Thank you for being so kind. I look forward to tonight."

I stared after her; it was the first time she had called any of our visits a *date*. My heart felt like a boy's toy ship bouncing up and down, held by one thin string. I wanted to snip the lifeline to reality and just let hope float! It didn't take long for the doubts to rush back in, however. She probably meant it as a *grandfatherly* date… something fun to do with an *old* person since she had nothing better to do this evening. *Was I replacing her late grandfather in our time together?* I still worried. I shoved the negative thoughts aside and dared to hope that she had said yes because she, too, felt a touch of the all-consuming spark I felt for her. If I could get up enough nerve to share my feelings, perhaps she'd share hers… it would be a pleasant evening regardless. *Who am I kidding?* I worried again. *If she doesn't have any feelings for me, I might as well kick the bucket here in Harlan and let them bury me by the lake!* The disappointment would be what snuffed out the candle flame completely.

After a light lunch at the café by myself, I stopped by the dress shop and inquired about Miss Atwood's taste in fashion. The female shoppers riffling through the racks looked a bit scandalized, but the owner, one robust and jovial Mrs. Penny, happily directed me to an exquisite blue dress in the window. "Anna Beth *loved* this one here – tried it on even," she said with a teasing voice as she held the dress up to herself and swayed back and forth in front of the mirror by the door. "Then she said, 'maybe nex' month, Penny!' n'lef' without buyin' a single thin'." The shop owner sighed as she hung it back up in the window. I chuckled, knowing a good saleswoman when I saw one.

"I'll take it, ma'am," I said with a smile.

"Well, I'll be – yer han'some *and* generous!" Mrs. Penny said, excitement shivering down her large frame as she danced to the register to ring up the purchase.

"You do great business here," I complimented, pulling out my wallet. Her whole face blushed as she thanked me profusely. "I was wondering – is there a way to deliver this dress to Miss Atwood at Carrie's house? She may want to wear it this evening," I added, sliding a fifty-dollar bill across the counter. That would pay for the dress and leave a sizable tip.

Mrs. Penny gasped and stuttered, "Well, o'course I… I can manage that!" She glanced at the gaggle of women still shooting me furtive looks, leaned across the counter, and cupped her mouth in her hand like she was going to tell me a secret. I leaned forward to hear her whisper like a schoolgirl. "Y'know, Mr. Johnston, I heard all 'bout y'two – how y've been spendin' so much time t'gether lately! Lot o'people don't think it's right, y'bein' such a… *gentleman* n'all. I want y't'know, though, I think Anna Beth Atwood is a peach, and hones'ly, love at any age is jus' wonderful! Don't pay y'no mind t'anyone else's opinions, y'hear?" she said sincerely.

I nodded, a bit confused, and noticed the other women scowl while exiting the store. I knew people were talking about us, but why would anyone think *I* was too good for *Anna Beth*? That was the most troubling thought of all Mrs. Penny had said. I cleared my throat. "I appreciate the advice, Mrs. Penny," I replied, helping myself to a piece of paper and pen from the corner of the counter. I quickly wrote a message for Anna Beth: *Looking forward to tonight*, folded the note, and handed it to the shop owner. "Can you include this when you drop off the package, please?"

"Sure can!" she said with a wink. "Ya'll have a lovely time!"

When I walked out of the shop, I took a deep breath of fresh air. I had the sense I had gotten myself into one good roller coaster of a ride with this girl from Harlan that I barely knew yet had fallen in love with. I shook every negative thought away and walked on down the road, forcing my mind toward more immediate matters… like whether to pick up my date in the Tin Lizzie or walk to her. I considered the extra time under the stars as an advantage of strolling through town, but I *had* implied that it would be a fancy night. If Anna Beth dressed up as I suspected, the car would be better suited for a woman in a nice dress and heels.

By six o'clock, I had donned my new suit, checked my tie twice in the mirror, and pep-talked myself that it was now or never to reveal my true feelings and intentions to the woman of my dreams. When I arrived at Carrie's home, nervous to the point of throwing up, Anna Beth didn't disappoint. That blue dress with the intricate lace work looked more beautiful on her that I could have ever imagined, and her blue heels matched perfectly! She had also piled her hair on top of her head in a picturesque bun with decorative pins sticking out of it. Stunning was a description for mere mortals; my angel was nothing short of divine.

Finding my voice, I said, "You look *amazing.*" I handed her the bouquet of flowers Carrie had generously helped me pick out. It was nice to know that at least Carrie – and Mrs. Penny – approved of Anna Beth and me spending time together.

"Thank you," she said, smelling the flowers with a little smile. Her face flushed, and she added quickly, "Thank you for the dress, too! I don't usually accept such extravagant gifts..."

"It was my pleasure, I assure you. I wanted you to have it – no strings attached," I replied, remembering how she liked to pay her own way. I suspected that was because men had tried to buy her affections or use her in some way in the past.

Her eyes drifted to the Tin Lizzie on the street, and she bounced up and down a little. "I've never ridden in a model-T! I've only traveled by train or stagecoach – and covered wagons when I was a little girl," she said with a chuckle.

"A covered wagon? You never told me you were *that* ancient," I teased. She playfully poked my arm with the flower stems, and warmth radiated out from the point of impact. It was going to be a fantastic night; I could feel it in my old bones.

I waited on the porch while she put the flowers in water, then we walked to the car. After opening the passenger side door for her, we talked over the roar of the engine all the way into town. I parked outside the theater and bought her popcorn and soda once inside. She insisted she didn't need any concessions, but I could tell she was secretly thrilled as she nursed the Pepsi-Cola and took great care not to drop even a kernel of popped corn.

"Have I told you how lovely you look tonight?" I asked, motioning her to two seats near the middle of the theater. She was looking all around the theater in sheer amazement as she sat down; it was the same way I was staring at her.

"Thank you, Mr. Johnston. I *feel* lovely tonight!" Anna Beth replied with a smile.

The lights dimmed, and I rested my arm on the back of her chair, leaving plenty of room for her to breathe. If there was one thing I had learned about women in all my years, it was not to rush a good thing.

I wanted her to know I was interested, but then allow her to make the next move forward.

"The owner assures me these are the best seats in the house," I leaned over and whispered.

"You talked with the owner of the theater?" she asked, surprised. Then a giggle slipped out. "Mr. Johnston! This is like a fairytale! The dress, the car, the popcorn and soda – you've done too much!" Someone hushed us from the row behind, and we both chuckled, settling in.

The opening credits finished rolling and the movie flashed onto the big screen. It was some comedy called *Animal Crackers* staring the Marx Brothers. Anna Beth gasped in delight to experience moving pictures, but I couldn't watch the movie for watching her from the corner of my eye. She felt all the emotions along with the actors and laughed out loud at all the right parts. I had an hour and a half to note every delicate muscle and line in her face, the outline of her lips, the curve of her nose – the gentle upward curl of her eye lashes. She had put just a touch of makeup on, too, even though she didn't need any. If this is what my parents' happiness together felt like – loving another person so completely and enjoying their company no matter what you were doing together – I was certain I had found what I had been seeking at last. I had thought I had it with Clara, but what I had felt for her was dull compared to my flourishing love for Anna Beth Atwood!

When the movie ended and the lights flickered on, I couldn't contain my fluttering emotion any longer. She looked at me breathlessly, no doubt about to thank me again for the novel experience, and I leaned in to kiss her before she had a chance to utter a word. My heart flooded with contentment as my lips pressed against hers. When I pulled back and opened my eyes, however, the shock on Anna Beth's face registered loud and clear, setting off alarm bells. My joy instantly sank into worry... like someone had poured cold water on the fireworks leaving a heavy, charred ball in the pit of my stomach. *Had I been mistaken in this whole endeavor?* I wondered frantically.

"Mr. Johnston!" Anna Beth gasped, her cheeks flushing red with embarrassment. She touched her lips and glanced around; other patrons were shuffling toward various exits, laughing, and talking amongst themselves. It was a small mercy no one was paying attention to us. "Mr. Johnston, I... I...." she stuttered and stood up abruptly. Her purse slid from her lap onto the floor, and we both leaned down for it, bumping our heads. She fumbled the strap over her shoulder as I hurried to my feet.

Wishing to apologize, I reached for her hand, but she backed up a step. "Anna Beth..." I pleaded with my hand still outstretched. "I'm sorry if I offended you. I just... you're just..." I searched for the right words, fearing I had just made an irreparable mistake.

"I'm so sorry, Mr. Johnston; I must go. I'm not feeling well all of sudden..." she mumbled while sidestepping into the aisle. I called to her to wait, to let me explain, but she bowed her head and got swallowed by the crowd pushing toward one of the back doors. By the time I made my own way out of the theater, she was nowhere to be seen.

Cursing myself, I got in my Tin Lizzie and slammed the door. *Why had I rushed her – us – whatever we were?* I criticized. *What do I do now? Go after her? Keep trying to explain how I accidentally and hopelessly fell in love with her, a woman almost a third my age? Would that help matters or make it all worse? Should I let her be and just slip out of town, never to face her rejection again?* I couldn't stomach the latter thought. Deep within myself something had shifted; I had never been truly happy gallivanting across the country, but at least I had been able to pretend. Now that I had a taste of real love, I wouldn't be content with anything less ever again. I sighed deeply, fired up the old model-T engine, and headed in the direction of Carrie's house. I had to find Anna Beth, and if she didn't want me, I'd live my time out like a prison sentence just waiting to die.

I searched both sides of the street as I slowly drove out of town, hoping I'd catch her walking. When I neared the hotel, I spotted Carrie waving to me from the covered porch. She wrapped her shawl tightly around her shoulders as I pulled in and rolled down my window. I watched her hurry down the steps and imagined she thought me senile – thinking a young woman in her prime could grow to have feelings for the washed-up version of what she deserved....

"Carrie, I messed up," I admitted right away, staring at my clenched hands on the steering wheel. They were shaking slightly. It had been a long time since I felt this kind of frustration and anger, and it all was directed inward.

"Mr. Johnston, listen, please," Carrie said quickly, resting an elbow on my window frame while simultaneously turning her back to a passing crowd of people out enjoying the evening. "This is *not* your fault."

I laughed ruefully and shook my head, ready to retort.

"I'm *serious* – Anna Beth was just here! She told me what happened at the theater. She was pretty upset," she confided. I glanced into Carrie's face for the first time and saw that her warm, green eyes were full of sympathy.

Running my fingers down my face with a sigh, I let my hands relax and fall in my lap. "And *how* is it not my fault?" I asked skeptically. "I must not have read her right. I thought... I'm *so* foolish to think..."

"There are things you don't know about Anna Beth Atwood," Carrie interjected quietly. "Things *she* has to tell you herself, in her own time... but I assure you, what happened tonight, how she reacted, it was *not* your fault."

I knew Anna Beth was a bit of a mystery, which I attributed to her parents' abandonment, but *what* would make her act so defensively? Carrie wasn't in the theater; she didn't see our interaction. I must have still looked doubtful because Carrie finally sighed, straightened up, and crossed her arms impatiently.

"Look, Mr. Johnston, I *know* she has feelings for you. She's told me that much," she said, taking the slow and deliberate tone one takes with a child who is not grasping a concept. "She's just learning how to love and be loved the way she deserves. That's the God's-honest truth of the matter... she needs more time is all."

As I stared at Carrie, trying to puzzle this mess out, the lakeside conversation about Anna Beth's little sister not being damaged flooded back to mind. A sickening feeling took hold in the pit of my stomach. *Why hadn't I realized it before?* I thought suddenly. *Something had happened to Anna Beth before she knew me; someone had hurt her so badly that she was still fighting the memory... like I sometimes fight the memory of warfare.* I was gripped with an urgency to find her, to love and protect her – if she'd only let me. "Where would she go?" I asked, my jaw set with renewed determination. "Would she go back to your house?"

Carrie shook her head and sighed. "I don't think so," she said, thinking quietly for a few moments. A thought dawned on her, and her eyes brightened. "You should try the church. That's where she went in times of trouble... when we were kids."

7

I drove to the church in the dark, the Tin Lizzie's feeble headlights the only illumination on the road out of town. Once past the schoolhouse, I saw the little white church on the hill. The low glow of candlelight was flickering in one of the windows; Carrie knew her friend well. With a steadying breath, I parked the car and made my way up the front steps. I hesitated only a moment before pulling open the door.

Anna Beth was hunched over on the front bench, her whole body shaking while she cried into her hands. She had lit a few candles around the piano, but the moonlight streaming in the windows blurred her figure like a halo around the edges. She looked back at the sound of the door creak, and her features came sharply into focus. Her eyes were red, and her delicate eye makeup just streaked down her cheeks. My heart wrenched within me to see her in such pain – my fallen angel in blue.

"Anna Beth?" I said quietly, slowly walking up the aisle. I worried any sudden movement or noise would frighten her off like a deer again. I paused several rows behind her. "Would you like some company? I'll leave if you'd rather…"

"Oh, Mr. Johnston," she choked out the word between sobs, "I've acted just *awful* this evening! I know you went through so much trouble to make it special. I'm truly sorry!" She yanked a handkerchief from her purse, leaving keys, money, and powder splayed on the bench in their wake, and wiped her eyes hard. I realized at that moment she was upset and angry with *herself*, not me.

I cleared my throat. "I think I'm the one who should be apologizing. I shouldn't have kissed you without asking permission. It was terribly forward of me. I'm sorry to have upset you so," I offered, pausing to search carefully for my next words. "It's just… it's been a long time since I had *real* feelings for someone. I guess I've forgotten the proper rules of courting."

Anna Beth chuckled, then mumbled, "I've made a glorious mess of things." She took a deep breath, tucking some fallen strands of hair behind her ear, and spoke more clearly. "It *wasn't* your kiss that upset me, Mr. Johnston; the kiss was truly lovely! It was just thoughts and feelings and memories from a *long* time ago that I knew I would have to face again one day." She shrugged in defeat. "I just didn't know it would be today, or that it would be with you." She looked up at me with timid eyes that begged me to understand. "The truth is, I've enjoyed my time with you more than I could ever express. Men my age do not seem to understand or want me, but *you* have been gentle, kind, and patient these last few months. If you can believe it, it has been exactly what I needed from a man." Her cheeks flushed slightly, and hope bubbled back up within me.

She enjoyed being with me; I was what she needed. I repeated her words to myself. *How long had I been searching for a place to belong with a purpose I could fulfill? I could live the rest of my life trying to be the man she needed and be content, if she would still have me.*

Anna Beth scooted over on the bench and patted the seat next to her. "I need to tell you something that happened to me a long time ago… something I've been struggling to get over once and for all," she said quietly. "You deserve to know why I ran out of the theater tonight."

I sat down. "I'm all yours," I said sincerely, ready to listen.

"It's pretty awful," she whispered, refusing to look me in the eye.

I thought of my time in the service, and my lips pressed together in a grim line. "I can handle awful," I assured her. "Sometimes we must because there's no other way forward."

She glanced at me only for a moment before taking a deep breath. "You know the Graingers that took in Livie and me when our family got to Harlan, right? Grace was kind and loving, but her husband was a cruel man," she began. "He treated people like he owned them, yet the whole town thought he was honest and good-natured. He beat Grace behind closed doors, and he worked me harder in the fields than any child should ever be worked." Anna Beth paused and looked sick to her stomach; her being so uncomfortable instantly made me uncomfortable. I had figured something terrible had happened to her but hearing the quiver in her voice filled me with dread.

"You don't have to talk about it if you don't want to," I offered. "I am in no way entitled to know your past." The urge to take her hand in mine was strong, but I feared to touch her when she felt so vulnerable and defensive.

"It's something you deserve to know, if you're going to know me at all," Anna Beth pressed on. I loved her more deeply for the courage. "We had been in their home for almost three years, and one night Mr. Grainger insisted I feed the chickens a second time. Now I look back and realize I should have known what was coming. I was only fourteen, though, and a sheltered fourteen at that. I was too naïve to understand his intentions when he followed me to the shed... but he took advantage of me that night and stole my innocence. Nothing has ever really been the same." She wrapped her arms around herself and dropped her chin. The pain that had lingered in her after all these years was tangible; it filled the sanctuary with a suffocating presence all its own.

I leaned forward, resting my head in my hands for a few moments, then sat up. "How could *anyone* do such a thing to another person... to a child, no less?" I asked, earnestly looking at Anna Beth. "I am so sorry that you had to suffer such an atrocity!"

She chewed the edge of her lip. "That's not all of it," she said quietly. "I ended up pregnant with his child. Carrie was the first person I told, and together we told our schoolteacher. Remember Mrs. Sensley? We thought she could help, but instead she spread rumors that the baby belonged to an older boy in class. A boy I despised, mind you." Anna Beth laughed scornfully at this detail and wrung her hands together in her lap.

"I was so angry with Grace for not standing up for me, but then I realized Mr. Grainger had broken her a long time before me. Imagine the whole town's surprise when he beat Grace and me black and blue – causing me to miscarry – and the sheriff was called. The truth finally came out that day. If it wasn't for Mr. Jingle..." her voice trailed off momentarily. "He saved our lives that day in more ways than one. I've been working ever since to not let what happened control me; that's why I came back to Harlan. I needed to see the place again, visit my baby's grave in this very churchyard... have a reckoning of sorts with my past... but as you can see, some days the past still reckons with me."

I finally held out my hand to her, and after a moment she extended her own to meet mine. Her fingers were small and soft as I cradled them gently, rubbing my thumb across her knuckles. "I can see why you've worked so hard to put it behind you, and how a night like tonight could have brought it all back to the forefront," I said quietly. "For me, sometimes it's sounds or smells that bring the war rushing back. I should have asked you before kissing you, regardless. I shouldn't have assumed..." I digressed while trying to center my thoughts. "Thank you for trusting me enough to share your whole story." Silence wrapped us in a warm embrace as we watched the candles flicker dancing light around the church.

Eventually, Anna Beth cleared her throat and looked my way again. "The truth is, Mr. Johnston," she said, her voice quavering as if it hurt to form the words, "I wasn't sure you'd *want* to know me anymore after you knew what all has happened. I know I'm... I'm *spoiled* in a sense, and you wouldn't be the first man who decided it best to walk away." Fresh tears filled her eyes again.

I now fully understood why she considered herself damaged, and I loathed the men who first put that thought in her mind. Instinctively, I reached for her with both arms, and she crumpled into my shoulder with a sob that shook her suddenly fragile frame. I pulled her close, wanting to cocoon her in my love and protect her from the outside world.

"I dated a man in North Carolina, where I taught for about two years, and I thought he loved me," she confided through her tears, "but when I finally told him the truth about my past, he didn't want me anymore. There were others before him, too, who only wanted a piece of me. No one has *ever* been interested in taking the whole of me that the good Lord put back together!" She paused, lifting her head as our eyes met. "I figured when I told you..."

I quickly put a finger to her mouth, not wanting to hear another word. "If those men didn't want the epitome of dignity, it was *their* loss... for that is what you are, Anna Beth Atwood – the cream of the crop," I assured her, brushing her soft lips with my thumb while cupping her cheek in my hand. "You may have had horrible things happen *to* you, but it isn't *who* you are. It's just part of your story, a chapter that helped shape you into the woman I see today... the woman I *love* with all my heart."

My angel in blue gasped and pulled out of my hands, her expression cautiously hopeful yet still wary. I chuckled softly; for being taken advantage of so early in life, she was still innocent in so many ways.

"I'd really like to kiss you again… properly this time. Is that okay?" I asked. I waited for her to lean toward me, which she did after a few moments, and I leaned forward to meet her. Our lips touched, and I kissed her as gently as I could. When she slowly kissed back, that familiar warmth renewed, tingling all over. When we pulled apart, I didn't see the dismayed and confused face from the theater any longer; in contrast, Anna Beth was smiling tenderly, her fingers wandering up to touch her lips.

"That was nice," she said, a little smirk tugging one corner of her mouth upward. "Thank you."

"Thank *you*," I replied, already worrying if we continued to sit close, I would seize the opportunity to kiss her again. I stood to restrain the urge and stretch my back a bit, and Anna Beth watched me walk back and forth in the altar of the church.

"While we're being honest with one another," I continued, venturing out on a limb as this seemed like the night to do such things, "*I* was convinced a young lady like *you* would never be interested in an old man like *me*. We are fifty years apart in age, you know, and I've done some pretty awful things in the past, although I know I'd be a better man for you. People will talk if our friendship continues to grow, though."

Anna Beth laughed fully, joy seeping back into her voice. "Age doesn't matter to me, Mr. Johnston, and your past is your past. We all make mistakes. It's a person's heart, mind, and future, how we work to better ourselves, that capture my attention… and if it's gossip that concerns you, I've been the source of people's conversation more times than I can count. I've learned to shed their words like water off a duck's back. I came back to Harlan to clear my head and heart once and for all, and I've rediscovered that all I want in life is joy and happiness. That doesn't have an age limit, does it?"

Thoughts and emotions tumbled through me faster than I could grasp them. I was a wandering bachelor for so many years, running from war and betrayal, searching for a life worth living, and now I somehow found myself in a church house with the most beautiful and compassionate woman I had ever met who was as interested in *me* as I was her! She didn't care about my money as so many others had; she, too, was just looking for a companion. I could tell that, to Anna Beth Atwood, love was *timeless* – and one persistent desire kept resounding in my heart and mind. *I wanted to live whatever time I had left on this earth with this woman! What was my life without her love?* I considered.

I dropped to one knee before cowardice took root again and took her hand in mine. *There's no turning back now*, I told myself. "Anna Beth Atwood," I said as she covered her mouth with her free hand. "Will you marry me and make me the happiest old man in the whole forty-eight states?" I asked.

Slowly, a grin spread across her face, and she nodded. "Yes, Mr. Johnston – proudly!" Anna Beth replied. She started to giggle, and her laugh was contagious. I stood up, pulling the woman of my dreams into my arms again. I held her close as we kissed a second time… or third if you counted the theater fiasco. It struck me again how I never wanted to let go of her.

"You will not be sorry, my angel," I whispered in her ear. "I know I probably don't have many years left, but I'll do right by you. We can live comfortably, and I'll buy you the finest things – anything you want! You don't have to work if you don't want to, but if you want to…"

She pulled back to look me in the eyes and placed her finger on my lips this time. With a wink, *she* leaned in and kissed *me*. I would have said I'd died and went to heaven, but I didn't want to tempt fate! It was enough to know that I was luckier than a hundred young men – to win the heart of Dignity.

8

The next day, I wrote a letter announcing our engagement to my buddy, Elliott. He was the only person I hoped could attend the wedding on my side, so I had also asked him to be my best man. About a week later, I impatiently asked Carrie to use the hotel phone so I could call the mercantile in Highland County, Virginia – the last town I knew him to have lived. It was like striking gold when the gentleman said Elliott was still a resident and he could relay the message! After another two excruciating days of waiting, Elliott finally called back on the hotel line; if I was a crying man, I would have shed tears to hear his voice after so long.

"I *just* now received your letter, Daniel," his voice teased through the old, crackly phone line. "You didn't even give me a chance to respond properly!"

"Well, I'm not getting any younger, you know," I joked back. Elliott laughed heartily.

"Ain't that the truth – you impatient, old coot! Where'd you dig up this pretty, young woman to marry this late in life, anyway?" he asked skeptically.

I sat quietly for a few moments before answering. "It's different this time, Elliott. I've never felt this way before, not even with Clara. I want to rise to the occasion and be the man she deserves," I finally said. We talked for half an hour, and, by the end of the call, the comrade that had pulled me out of battle and saved my life was eager to come to Harlan and support the union.

Elliott arrived by train two weeks later. Anna Beth and I were waiting at the station when he stepped down from the train in his brown suit, carrying a hardcover suitcase. I firmly shook his hand then wrapped him in a quick, tight embrace. He slapped my back in greeting.

I leaned back and took a good look at him. It had been many years since we set eyes on each other. He looked good with a tidy, trimmed beard and mustache, both graying alongside his short hair. "My *old* friend!" I jeered, knowing full well he was five years my junior. "Time has *not* been kind to you!"

Elliott scoffed. "You have room to talk," he teased, "I was going to say *you're* finally starting to look your age!" We roared with laughter and embraced once more, holding on a bit longer this time.

"Seriously, Daniel," Elliott continued, pulling away and slipping his hands in his jacket pockets, "you look great." He glanced at Anna Beth and nodded politely. "Now, *who* is this you've gone and pulled into your web?" he asked, smirking. I introduced my best friend to the love of my life, and he took her hand gently in his. Anna Beth's cheeks flushed as he bowed to kiss the back of it.

"You don't know what you're getting into with this one," Elliott whispered as he stood up, motioning to me. It was now my turn to punch him in the arm, just like old times. Anna Beth smiled mischievously.

"Don't you worry, Mr. Foster – I can handle him," she replied confidently. With a hearty chortle, Elliott reached up to rub his beard.

"Uh-oh, Daniel, I think you finally met your match with this one!" he said, his eyes twinkling as I reached for his suitcase and pointed them both toward the Tin Lizzie on the street.

"Come on, Elliott, let's get you settled into the hotel. We can have supper in their dining room… I'm sure you're starved after that long train ride," I offered, opening the passenger door. Anna Beth motioned for Elliott to sit up front, and, after a short argument, he graciously accepted the hospitality.

"When did you start driving a tin can on wheels?" Elliott continued the banter once inside.

"Oh, don't get him started," Anna Beth groaned from the back seat. "He loves his Model-Ts!"

"I'll have you know these practical, little cars have won races all over the States! Haven't you heard of Noel Bullock and *Old Liz*? I was there my friend – I *witnessed* the upset," I said, defending my car choice proudly.

The conversation easily shifted to Harlan as Anna Beth pointed out different shops and buildings along the way, and, once inside the hotel, we introduced him to Carrie, Anna Beth's matron of honor. She showed him up the stairs and to the room next to mine while Anna Beth and I waited in the dining room for him to change clothes for dinner. By five-thirty, we were all seated for a delicious, home-cooked meal of fried chicken, mashed potatoes, and green beans – even Carrie, who rarely got to take a break from work.

Laughing and talking the night away, we told stories until we were the last table in the dining room. As night fell outside the windows, our attention turned to the wedding. It was just a few short days away now, but it felt like a lifetime of waiting. To me, it had been.

"Where will you all tie the knot?" Elliott asked, stirring cream into his second cup of coffee. I took a sip of my own, enjoying the warmth. With the dining room cleared out, the cool drafts were chilling me to the bone.

"Well, Anna Beth would've been married in the town church, but since I've been divorced and have a living wife, we decided the lake at sunset is the next best place," I said.

Elliott glanced at Anna Beth; I had watched him size her up all night, and I didn't begrudge his curiosity. I would have scrutinized any potential mate he desired, too, if given the chance. It was instinct for us. We had learned to protect each other in war so we both could survive to see another day. He cleared his throat and leaned forward, his elbows on the table. I knew what was coming and took a long sip of coffee.

"Now, little lady," Elliott said seriously, "I was only half joking earlier when I said you didn't know what you were getting into with this one." He looked her straight in the eyes, and she returned his stare unwaveringly. "Are you *really* going into this marriage eyes wide open? You, my dear, are a spring chicken, and he's an old rooster! I won't lie – it makes a man wonder why a young, pretty woman like yourself wouldn't just marry someone your own age."

Knowing Anna Beth's experiences with men, his words made me stir uncomfortably. I didn't want her to feel obligated to tell Elliott why finding companionship with men her own age had been such a challenge, nor did I want Elliott to give her reason for second thoughts regarding our union. I glanced at her anxiously, but relaxed when I saw a smile sneaking across her face.

"Well, Mr. Foster, it seems to me that *every* young, pretty woman needs a money bag in her back pocket!" she proclaimed. Carrie spit her water out as her face reddened to match her hair.

"Anna!" she chided, reaching for a napkin to clean up the mess.

I locked eyes with my betrothed, and we broke loose in laughter; we laughed until tears misted our eyes! Elliott had prodded at us all evening in jest, so it was a rightful turn of events for her to finally pay him back. Only when Elliott started chuckling did Carrie grin nervously, her cheeks still rosy with embarrassment for her friend.

"In all seriousness, Mr. Foster," Anna Beth continued as we all regained our composure, "yes, I *know* what I'm getting myself into. I know Mr. Johnston and I may not have many years together, and I know I may end up being more of a caregiver as we both age." She leaned forward, her eyes resolute. "I know he has faults as we all have, but he has been nothing but caring and respectful to me. I *love* Mr. Johnston. He filled a hole within me I've tried to fill for years... and no matter how big, small, young, or old, when God sends joy into your life, who are we to put conditions on it and say it's not good enough? I may never find this kind of love with a young man. I may never find it again after Mr. Johnston... so, I'm not going to pass it up even if it may only be for a short time."

"'Tis better to have loved and lost than never to have loved at all,'" Carrie quoted quietly.

I cleared my throat. "And who knows?" I asked. "I may outlive you all! Don't put me in the grave yet, old pal!"

We all laughed again, and Elliott held up his hands in surrender. "Okay, *okay*... she passed my test! You all have my stamp of approval," he said.

I had hoped he would feel this way, but I nonchalantly crossed my arms in mock disdain. "Like we *needed* your approval," I replied. I glanced at Anna Beth and winked; she was beaming with pride.

We soon retired, the men to our hotel rooms and the ladies to Carrie's house, and the following days flew by with wedding preparations. I didn't relish the excitement surrounding the wedding myself – I would have been fine with a preacher, the witnesses, my angel, and a couple of rings. However, I understood this was Anna Beth's first wedding and happily deferred to Carrie's expertise in making it an event to remember. It was her suggestion to set up a trellis with flowers by the lake, have a runner for Anna Beth to walk on, order bouquets from the floral shop...

all kinds of lady things I wouldn't have thought about on my own. I knew Anna Beth wouldn't have told me she desired them, either; she was meek that way. Carrie also enlisted the help of Mrs. Penny from the dress shop to make the wedding gown, but her *best* idea was helping me arrange for Anna Beth's family to come in town for the wedding!

It was the day before we were to take our vows, and my bride-to-be hadn't seen Grace, the woman who raised her and her youngest sister, Olivia, since Mr. Jingle's funeral. We awaited their arrival on the platform; Anna Beth bouncing on the balls of her feet as she stared down the empty tracks. I couldn't wipe the smile from my face; seeing her so excited gave me such deep joy.

"You told them I was old, right?" I teased. "Like *grandfather* old? I don't want anyone getting off the train and having a heart attack… especially me…"

"Mr. Johnston, will you *stop* that nonsense already!" Anna Beth said, playfully nudged my arm. "*Yes*, I told them you were older than me. Most importantly, I told them I *loved* you. That's all they'll care about anyway."

As the train came whistling into the station, she squealed with delight and clasped her hands together. The wheels screeched to a halt as steam belched from the engine's stacks. Doors opened, spilling passengers onto the sidewalk. I was the first to spot an older woman, thin with graying blonde hair neatly pulled back into a bun, step from the train and look around expectantly. A girl of about fifteen with bouncy blonde locks got off right behind her. I nudged Anna Beth and pointed in their direction.

"That's them!" Anna Beth declared. "Grace! Olivia!" She waved a handkerchief in the air, attracting their attention. With huge smiles, they waved back and began to push through the crowd to meet us. As soon as they were within arms' reach, the women dropped their luggage and engulfed Anna Beth in a hug; the older one wiped her own tears. "I'm *so* happy to see you two!" Anna Beth finally said, pulling back to look them up and down.

Grace tenderly brushed a strand of hair from Anna Beth's face; if a person didn't know she was her foster mother, they would never suspect the two women weren't related – they looked very much like mother and daughter. "It's so good t'be here, sweetheart," she answered.

Olivia, the youngest of the trio, shook with such excitement I expected her to burst any moment. "We have a surprise fo' ya, Anna

Beth!" she squealed. "It's a *good* one, too... y'won't b'lieve it – not n'a million years!"

Like the girl's, Grace's eyes also sparkled with childlike mischievousness. Anna Beth watched them curiously as they stepped apart, revealing three more women walking toward us with their suitcases. I looked from the approaching women's faces to Anna Beth's face and back again, realizing who they were only a fraction of a second before she did. The realization dawned on Anna Beth suddenly, like a light bursting into existence, and she grabbed Olivia's arm for support. I instinctively took hold of her other arm to steady her.

"Do y'recognize us?" the woman in the middle asked with a smirk. She had shoulder-length, dull brown hair and lackluster features, but her spunky personality made up for it. "We *are* all grown up, after all."

"*Janie?*" Anna Beth whispered. Her eyes shifted to the next woman who was slightly taller with softer features but obviously more timid. "*Emily?*" she asked in disbelief. Anna Beth's eyes shone with tears as she looked to the oldest of the three. "*Martha?*"

The five sisters, reunited after so many years and miles, became overwhelmed with emotion as everyone else wandered from the platform. Only Grace and I understood how miraculous of a moment this truly was; most of the women hadn't seen each other in thirteen years. That was like a lifetime – each sister had changed so much; they were branches reaching in all different directions with only the roots in common.

In an instant, my thoughts ran back to my children in Oregon. *They've surely grown and changed, too,* I considered, even though they would forever be frozen in time in my mind. I loved and missed them every day, but my previous life seemed a whole world away now. My existence was fully here with the woman I had been destined for all along.

"I can't believe it!" Anna Beth sobbed into her handkerchief, bringing me back to the present. "How... how did you..."

"I still had y'address fo' Martha at home," Grace said with a smile. "I got in touch with 'er right after we heard the good news, n'she n'Janie did the rest! They traveled from Missouri t'Tennessee t'visit with Olivia n'I first, then we all stopped by Emily's town n'picked her up on the way here. Weddin's're perfect fo' reunions, don't y'think?" This woman, who I knew had suffered so much at her husband's hand, radiated such earnest warmth and love. I could see how Anna Beth was able to overcome her own troubled childhood and grow into the woman I knew and loved with Grace as her example.

Anna Beth nodded and hugged Grace's neck, then she embraced each of her sisters one at a time. When she circled back toward me, she laughed and hugged me tightly as well. "All of this happened because *you* loved me," she whispered in my ear. I gently patted her back and smiled at her family. None of them understood that all of this was happening because *she* loved me, but I did.

"Well, this is quite the surprise," I said with a chuckle. "Hello, everyone, I'm Daniel Johnston."

"Oh, good heavens – forgive me!" Anna Beth laughed, wiping her face dry with the handkerchief. "This is my fiancé, Mr. Johnston." She pointed out each woman to me in turn. "This is Grace, the woman who took me in; Martha, my oldest sister; Janie and Emily – they might as well have been twins," she added with a chuckle. "And this is Olivia, my baby birthday sister; she and I stayed together after our parents left." Everyone nodded politely as we exchanged pleasantries.

"I'm sure you all are tired from your journey. How about we head to the hotel to get everyone settled and have lunch at the café?" I suggested.

Anna Beth hooked her arm through mine as we led the way to the hotel, and Carrie cried to see her best friend coming with *all* her sisters and Grace behind her. She came out from behind the desk and hugged each of them. "I know you all don't really know me," she sniffed, "except Grace and Olivia, that is… but I feel like I know every one of you!" She hugged Anna Beth extra tightly. When she handed the women their room keys and they started up the stairs, Anna Beth glanced at me uncertainly.

I nodded for her to join them. "Go ahead and help them unpack," I told her. "I'll meet you at the café – take your time." She kissed my cheek and hurried after her family, passing Carrie who was hurrying back down the steps to the ringing phone.

The call was quick, and when she hung up, I said, "One more day, my friend! Can you believe she said yes?"

Carrie dabbed at her eyes with a soft laugh. "It's *just* like her, really. She was always doing things that surprised folks when we were kids. She's got such a good heart, Mr. Johnston; I think you all make a great couple," she replied, glancing up the stairs lovingly. "It is *so* good to see her with her family!"

"You should join us for lunch if you can get away… my treat," I offered. "You're like another sister to her anyway." Carrie accepted graciously and disappeared to the back apartment to get one of her parents to take over the front desk. "See you there!" I called after her with a grin.

Elliott was waiting for me outside the café, and he told me of the morning he spent exploring Harlan while we waited on the womenfolk. After they came walking across the street like a gaggle of geese, we all gathered inside, the waitress pulling tables together. The lunch conversation quickly turned to the retelling of their fascinating family history – how the parents had brought all of them but Martha, the oldest, to the coal mountains of Kentucky for a better life but ended up leaving them in foster care. I learned in greater detail what happened to each sister after they were separated; they were all married now, except Anna Beth who would be tomorrow, and Olivia, who was looking at nursing colleges for women.

They soon asked about my story, and I was honest without placing blame since there was plenty to go around concerning my past. I explained how I had come home from war a different man, and my first wife and I couldn't make the marriage work any longer. We divorced, and I took to traveling. I added that the only person who kept me from moving on to the Gulf, where I planned to live out my last days, was their beautiful sister, the angel of the post office.

"Aw," Emily and Olivia cooed to each other. "What a sweet way t'meet!" Emily affirmed.

"*Angel?*" Janie asked skeptically, raising one eyebrow. "Are we talking about the same person? D'ya know she continu'lly told me nothin' was my business n'kicked me awake jus' 'bout ev'ry mornin'?"

Martha, the oldest sister who took Janie in after she ran away from her foster home in Harlan, slapped her younger sister's arm. "Janie! Y'should be ashamed of y'self!" she chided. Janie just laughed and winked at Anna Beth.

"Geez, Martha – she knows I'm jus' kiddin'," Janie replied with a grin, rubbing her arm.

"You deserved it," Anna Beth retorted, her words with a playful lilt of their own.

"I tell you what," Elliott chimed in, jabbing his thumb at me. "It must have been love at first sight to make this old guy slow down. For eleven years now, I've received letters from *all over* the states. He hardly stayed in one place long enough for me to return one!" We all laughed as I rested my hand on Elliott's shoulder.

"The funny thing is that I used *you* and our letters as an excuse to go to the post office and see Anna Beth every day!" I confessed. "I don't know what other reason I could have given to show up as often as I could, so I guess it's fair to say you saved my life twice now!"

By the time we finished our dessert, it was early evening. Carrie had been clear about the girls needing their time to rest and get ready, so I knew I wouldn't see Anna Beth again until she walked down the aisle by the lake. I hung back at the café door, waiting for her to pass, and kissed her goodnight before watching her walk across the street, arm in arm with Janie and Emily. Atop of feeling her contentedness, knowing she was about to be mine made my heart surge in a way I thought no longer possible.

Elliott cleared this throat and slapped me on the back. "There's still some daylight left, my friend. Let's go fishing," he said. "You'll see her tomorrow, and remember, this time it's till *death* do you part!"

"Hey, now," I retorted with a laugh, walking down the steps next to him. "The old man jokes are getting *old*."

"This coming from the king of old man jokes?" Elliott asked, drawing back like he was shocked. He shook his head and spoke in a more serious tone, "I still don't see how a woman like *that* fell for a guy like *you*, but I'm glad she did, pal. It's good to see you put down roots and be happy again."

"It's good to *feel* happy again and *want* to put down roots," I agreed. I didn't say it to Elliott, but I had surprised even myself. Every day I woke up and had to remind myself this wasn't all just a dream.

Elliott must have planned the fishing trip because he had stowed two poles and a tackle box around the corner of the café. By the time we walked the short distance to the lake, the sun was just beginning to set over the coal mountains, dashing the sky with strokes of yellow, burnt orange, and fiery red. It was a fitting way to end a wonderful evening.

"So, do you have any worries?" Elliott asked, casting his baited line into the still water. It plunked out in the middle and disrupted the surface with perfect ringlets.

"What do you mean?" I asked, feeling a tug on my already submerged line. I jerked it, but the fish managed to steal my bait without getting hooked. With a grunt of disappointment, I reeled it in, rebaited, and cast again.

"Worries about the wedding and all... what life is going to be like after," he pressed. "I'm the best man, you know; I figure we're supposed to talk about pre-wedding jitters so you can go in tomorrow confident and in charge."

"That sounds like a bunch of woman-talk right there!" I said with a laugh.

Elliott shrugged innocently. "Well, I imagine her matron of honor and family are putting her jitters to rest as we speak!" he replied.

I glanced at my friend, who had turned his attention back to his line, and felt a rush of gratitude that he would drop everything to come to my wedding after all these years. When you go to war with somebody and share the feelings of fear, exhaustion, loneliness, and best of all, camaraderie, it bonds you together in ways you can never quite explain. I decided his question deserved my utmost sincerity.

"Well, I know we love each other and are good for each other," I said quietly. "I have plenty of money to buy her whatever she wants, and I'm not worried about how much time we have together because, to tell you the truth, any time spent with her is a gift I don't really deserve."

"So, what *are* you worried about? Everyone worries about something," Elliott inquired again, jerking his line. "Drat – I think another got away."

I gathered my thoughts as he reeled in the bobber, worm still attached, and recast. *How honest did I want to get with him? How honest did I want to be with myself?* I wondered. Surely, he would understand things generally not spoken aloud – since we were both old men. I cleared my throat nervously. "I guess the only thing that nags at me is, you know, wondering whether I can *please* her the way a husband should his wife. I can joke about being old until the cows come home, but that's the only part of my old self I wish was young again. I'm not too sure of myself when it comes to pleasing a woman anymore."

Elliott nodded knowledgeably, his face solemn. "That my friend, I understand... it happens to the best of us as our bodies slow down. But you know what? You've kept yourself in pretty good shape; besides, I don't think she's the type to care one way or another. I've seen the way she looks at you. She wants to be your *companion*, the woman you love – and love comes in many forms."

I chewed on that thought awhile, remembering a time when intimacy was of the utmost importance to me. A lot had changed since I left Clara. My priorities had shifted these last several years, and like Anna Beth had told Elliott the first night, she knew what she was getting into when she said yes to marrying an older man. I decided I had no cause to worry about something outside my control; she was going into this with eyes as wide open as my own. Elliott was right; love does come in many forms.

We fished a while longer, dusk settling around us as the eventual ebb and flow of our conversation turned to the old days when we fought side by side. We shared what we knew, if anything, of the comrades who had enlisted with us. Some had gotten married, others had families, a few worked odds-and-ends jobs. A couple couldn't handle the world after war and had taken their own lives. Others were shell-shocked; they never stopped fighting the war in their minds and ended up institutionalized for their own safety and that of others. That hit close to home for me as I had also spent some time in a mental institution with many of the same thoughts; thankfully, however, I survived the experience and got straightened out well enough. Lastly, we talked about those who never made it home. We gave their memories a few minutes of silence in respect of the ultimate sacrifice; a sacrifice that we ourselves had just narrowly escaped.

"Are you going to let your children know where you are and that you're remarrying?" my friend asked after a long pause.

I watched our bobbers out on the lake and shook my head. I had thought about writing my children many times over the years and still figured they didn't want to hear from me. Anna Beth encouraged me to reconnect with my children every time the subject came up in conversation, but our family situations were just different. Her parents left with the promise to come back and seemingly disappeared; my children knew I walked out on them and didn't return on purpose. If I was being honest with myself, I reckoned part of my obstinance was also fearfulness. *What if all they wanted was to hear from me like Anna Beth wanted to hear from her parents? What if I reached out, tried to explain why I had to leave, and I still wasn't good enough?*

"I don't think I can bring myself to contact them, Elliott," I admitted. "Most of them have grown into adults now, anyway. The younger ones probably don't even remember me. When I left, I feel like I took the right to know them – or them know me – away from all of us. It's one of my biggest regrets in life, but I don't believe the rift can ever be bridged."

Elliott sighed, reeling in his line a bit. "Relationships of any kind can get messy, but I *don't* think that means people stop caring. No, sir. I'm sure they still care about you as I know you do them; it's just natural. Maybe one day you can see a way across the divide again."

It soon got too dark to see our poles, and we quietly walked back to the hotel by moonlight. After climbing the stairs, I noticed the girls' rooms down the hall were quiet and wondered if the bridal party was asleep in there. Perhaps they had moved the fun to Carrie's house so as not to disturb other patrons....

"I'm sure they're taking good care of her," Elliott said, patting me on the back sympathetically. "Get some sleep, Daniel." I nodded as we bid each other good night with a firm handshake. "One more night," he added with a grin, squeezing my hand.

"One more night," I replied with a chuckle. We unlocked our own rooms, and I closed the door behind me, leaning against it with a sigh. My back and legs were tired from the day's activities, but it was a satisfied kind of tired.

I shuffled to the little bathroom to wash up, deciding it best to save the shaving of my face until the morning. Then I changed into my pajamas, climbed into the bed, and let my muscles finally relax. *This is the last night I'll sleep alone*, I thought. *Tomorrow, I'll be married... to a girl a third my age*. It was certainly unusual, but unusual doesn't have to be wrong. Unusual can be beautiful, like a movie where star-crossed lovers find a way to defeat all odds and be happy together. Other people might not see it like we do; many probably won't understand how we could fall in love. They may wonder if it is love or some other convenience. I let my mind wander to the justifications they'd think of... *Anna Beth could be looking for a wealthy man to support her, and I for a young woman to care for me in my old age*. I knew in my heart that was not the truth, however. *This is love*. An amazing, deep, miraculous love maybe only we ourselves would ever fully understand the power of.

My eyes closed with heaviness as I took a deep breath, succumbing to rest as my thoughts slowed to a trickle. *This is nothing short of a miracle. That's why I stopped in Harlan on a whim and met Anna Beth at the post office, why she somehow grew to have feelings for me whilst I loved her at first sight. It was a miracle*. I wasn't a religious man by any stretch of the imagination, although I did pray to Him a few times when I felt the chances of survival on foreign soil were slim. I think most young soldiers do reach for any notion of higher power when in the trenches of war or life. I wondered – seriously – if God had heard my heart's yearning now as I assumed He had then. "Thank you, God," I whispered into the darkness right before I drifted into sleep. "Thank you for being merciful to someone as undeserving as me."

9

When dawn peeked through the curtains and lit up my small hotel room with the glow of new possibilities, I would have jumped out of bed in excitement if I had been young. Instead, I propped myself up on one elbow, threw the covers back, and swung my legs over the bed slowly. My joints popped as I pushed myself up, and I hoped the morning sounds I had grown accustomed to wouldn't bother Anna Beth. I walked out the tightness in my hips while rotating my shoulders a few times, then went on about my morning routine. Elliott would be waiting for me to join him for breakfast in the dining room downstairs in less than half an hour.

My friend was already at a table drinking his morning coffee when I walked in. He wiggled his eyebrows at me and grinned. "Big day today! Are you *sure* you don't want to back out? You still have time to change your mind, you know," he jeered.

I sat down across from him and ordered a coffee from the waitress. "I hope Anna Beth's ladies aren't giving her the same advice," I replied with a grimace. Elliott chuckled and stroked his beard for a moment.

"It's going to be a *great* day, my friend! I can feel it," he said, nodding encouragingly. The waitress brought my coffee, and we ordered breakfast.

I took a long sip from the cup and sighed. I said, "That's more like it – I guess I'll still let you be my best man." Elliott and I grinned at each other; in a few short hours, I would be a married man! *Surely this time, with this woman, I could do it right*, I thought to myself.

We talked about a myriad of things over our hearty breakfast of pancakes, sausage, and eggs, then retired to our rooms to get ready for the afternoon. Carrie had threatened she would knock me out and I'd miss the whole thing if I dared come out of the hotel before it was time for the wedding. She had gotten a lot more comfortable with jesting and thought it very funny to say to me that she would marry her best friend off to a *younger man who could follow the rules.* Sometimes it's the quiet ones you must watch out for, but with the way she loved Anna Beth, I figured I best listen!

So, after donning my suit, there I sat on the edge of my bed. My hair was slicked back, my face clean-shaven, and my hands clasped in my lap. Occasionally, I would dry my sweaty palms on the knees of my pants. One would think after seventy-five years of living I'd have mastered my nerves, but the current situation begged to differ. *What if she got cold feet and didn't come to the lake?* I worried. *What if we got into the marriage and she realized I really couldn't keep up with her? Would she regret the whole thing as a huge mistake? What if I died next week and widowed her too young? People would criticize her and say she only married me to gain what was left of my fortune.* I shook my head, stood up, and paced the small room. Thankfully, a knock broke the silence that was suffocating me with concern.

"How about a game of cards?" Elliott asked when I opened the door. He looked good in his suit and, as always, was right on time when I needed him most. I followed him back down to the dining room, and we played a few rounds of cards over another cup of coffee each.

"Did you hear about the trouble coming to Harlan?" he asked quietly, not looking up from his hand.

I took a sip of coffee, letting the warm liquid soothe my nerves. I knew exactly what he was talking about but had tried not to think about it. The stock market crash a few years back had run the economy into the ground, and now there were a series of skirmishes over coal mining labor laws stirring up the town. The coal miners and union organizers were on one side of the debate with the coal firms and law enforcement on the other. It had something to do with better wages and working conditions in the mines... as it always does. Strikes were inevitable, and with strikes would inevitably come protests and violence.

"I've heard the rumors," I replied simply. Elliott flipped a card to the middle of the table as I continued to examine my hand.

"So... what's the plan for after the wedding?" he asked. "Are you all going to settle here in Harlan with all this trouble brewing? It could be a long and nasty affair if you ask me."

"If the federal troops have to come in and occupy the county to keep the peace, that will turn ugly," I agreed with a frown. "We're leaving town for an extended honeymoon, though, so we will have time to figure out where to settle after... I'll buy her a house anywhere she wants to live, but I do hope it's not here. She has history here that is better off left behind her anyway." I hadn't told Elliott about Anna Beth's childhood trauma, but I knew a thing or two about staying where the ghosts of past can easily torment you. I had managed to move on in my own life, and I hoped after today she would be able to as well.

Elliott glanced at the clock on the wall and his mischievous grin reappeared. The joker never could stay serious for very long. "It's about that time," he said, laying his cards down to reveal he had been bluffing his hand the whole time. He laughed at my stunned expression. "Come on, you old, gullible goat... let's go get your ball and chain on!"

Leaving the hotel, we marched shoulder to shoulder to the lake, the rigid routines of military service still engrained years later. I had longed to see Anna Beth all morning, even for just a moment, but I didn't know if seeing her would have settled or intensified my giddy schoolboy feelings. *After tying the knot and celebrating, we will leave Harlan and be together from this day forward – come what may.* The thought made my heart nearly thump out of my chest.

Elliott and I took our places by the water's edge, and I admired the vines of blue and purple flowers entwined around the trellis. We couldn't have asked for a better day; it was clear and sunny, and the lake's calm waters glittered in the light. I had paid for Carrie to book a string quartet from a few towns over, and Elliott patted me on the back as music filled the air. Various town folk were gathering as we stood still. Many of them I knew cared about Anna Beth, and the rest, I figured, were here out of curiosity. I tried not to think about their judgmental opinions, instead focusing on the bond I knew Anna Beth and I mutually shared. When the county judge joined us under the trellis, Elliott checked his pocket watch and whistled.

"It's about time, my friend," he said quietly. I took a deep breath and smoothed down my suit jacket, feeling around the front to make sure I had buttoned it appropriately. I must have let my hand linger over my chest a moment too long because Elliott added, "Now is not the time to have a heart attack, okay?"

We both chuckled until I saw the crowd of women emerge from the café. Breath caught in my throat as I straightened my back, scanning the group for my bride. The string quartet changed songs as Carrie separated herself from the huddle. With a long purple dress rippling in the breeze and her red hair in ringlets, she slowly made her way down the path toward us. She winked at me as she took her place and then whispered, "Don't forget the runner!"

The one job I had been assigned, besides the proverbial *I do*, rushed back to the forefront of my mind. I thanked her with a nod and elbowed Elliott. Together, we each took a corner of the white runner that lay in folds at our feet and slowly stretched it out toward the café. Anna Beth's long-lost sisters, Martha, Janie, and Emily, were smiling at us as we approached. I glanced at the café, wondering if Anna Beth was as nervous and excited as I was. The song played until we took our spots back under the trellis, then the musicians changed to the final piece – *The Wedding March*.

Martha, Janie, and Emily stepped aside to let Olivia walk up the aisle alone. She was wearing the same purple dress as Carrie, and I grinned at her blonde curls bouncing with every step. She was no longer a little girl, but it was still fitting to have her trail the flower petals her older sister would walk on. Those two had endured much heartbreak, and together, they had survived. I smiled when she took her place next to Carrie, and then looked back to see Anna Beth, my angel, walking down the aisle arm-in-arm with Grace.

Mrs. Penny stood in the audience dabbing her eyes as Anna Beth walked by; the love she had put into every stitch of that wedding gown was evident. The dress was white with lace sleeves, and little beads that sparkled in the light adorned the bodice. The hem, while barely touching the ground in the front, gave way to an exquisite train. Anna Beth's lightly tanned skin looked soft, like warm butter, and her golden-brown hair was twisted and folded in an elegant swirl atop her head. A lacey veil hid her face, but I could just make out her almond-shaped eyes and the curves of her soft lips. My morning fears of being stood up at the altar fled away; there was no hint of reservation in her features at all.

As my wife-to-be seemingly floated toward me, my heart picked up a new cadence. I didn't hear the music anymore or even feel the breeze on my face… my only acknowledgement was of her. Tears leaked from my eyes, and I hastily took a handkerchief from my pocket to wipe them away. As the women slowed to a stop in front of the trellis, Grace reached out and tenderly squeezed my arm. Her smile was both compassionate and joyful. She played the part of a proud mother well, and I got her message loud and clear – *Take care of my little girl.*

The judge cleared his throat and began. "Dearly beloved, we are gathered here today to witness the union of Mr. Daniel Johnston and Miss Anna Beth Atwood in holy matrimony, which is an honorable estate that is not to be entered into unadvisedly or lightly but reverently and soberly. If anyone can show just cause why they may not be lawfully joined together, let them speak now or forever hold their peace," he spoke. I stared at Anna Beth, barely registering his words. She was going to be mine; she had chosen *me*! "Who gives this woman to be married to this man?" the judge continued after a short pause.

"Her sisters and I do," Grace said confidently. She lifted Anna Beth's veil just enough to kiss her cheek then took my hand and intertwined it with my bride's. The delicate touch of Anna Beth's fingers wrapped in mine brought back memories of the night at the church when we bared our souls to each other. I rubbed her knuckles with my thumb, wondering if she felt the same electricity. *"Be good to her, Daniel,"* Grace instructed.

I tore my gaze from Anna Beth long enough to look into Grace's eyes. "I will," I promised earnestly. "You can be sure of that." Grace patted our hands and then resumed her place among the sisters, the last three of whom had walked to the front row to watch the ceremony.

The judge nodded at me, and I listened carefully to his next words. "Repeat after me, Mr. Johnston," he said, "I take you, Anna Beth, to be my lawfully wedded wife from this day forward, for better, for worse, for richer, for poorer, in sickness and in health, to love and to cherish, and to honor, till death do us part, according to God's holy ordinance; and thereto I give thee my troth." I repeated each phrase and held my breath when he turned to Anna Beth.

"I take you, Daniel Johnston," she repeated after him in turn, "to be my lawfully wedded husband from this day forward, for better, for worse, for richer, for poorer, in sickness and in health, to love and to cherish, and to obey, till death do us part, according to God's holy ordinance; and thereto I give thee my troth." She smiled under her veil and squeezed my hand.

Elliott and Carrie handed our rings to the judge as he continued. "The wedding ring is an outward sign of an inward bond which unites two loyal hearts in endless love. It is a seal of the vows Daniel and Anna Beth have made to one another. May he and she who give and wear them live together in unity, love, and happiness for the rest of their lives."

He gave the rings to us, and we took turns slipping them on each other's fingers.

"With this ring, I thee wed," I spoke first.

"With this ring, *I* thee wed," she answered. I chuckled, loving both her humility and preference to have the last word.

"By the powers vested in me by the Commonwealth of Kentucky, I now pronounce you man and wife. You may kiss your bride," the judge announced. "Ladies and gentlemen, I present to you Mr. and Mrs. Daniel Johnston!"

The crowd erupted in a round of applause, and with a mixed sigh of relief and anticipation, I lifted the veil over Anna Beth's head. Finally, there she was in full! *No angel in heaven can hold a candle to my Mrs. Anna Beth Johnston*, I thought to myself as I leaned in to kiss her. The memory of taking comfort in one another's arms in the church house rushed back; nothing felt more right in my whole life.

Elliott whistled as we pulled apart, and Carrie and Grace both wiped their tears. Anna Beth smiled up at me, and I wrapped her in a hug as we turned together to face the cheering crowd. The quartet started a joyous song as we walked up the aisle and on to the hotel where the reception would be held, the whole town following behind us. Having the woman I loved in the near winter of my life on my arm was the happiest moment I could ever remember.

Carrie's parents had transformed the dining room into a reception hall with streamers, balloons, and tiered cake; we had a fantastic celebration! I had hired a photographer, an extravagant splurge that added extra magic to the special occasion, and he took several pictures of us and our wedding party. I requested him to also get a few of Anna Beth with Grace and her sisters. I wanted her to cherish the memory of their reunion alongside our union for the rest of her life. We visited with family and friends for more than two hours, but when the sun started to drop behind the mountains, Anna Beth excused herself with Grace to get changed. We would leave for our honeymoon, the destination of which I had kept a secret, when she was ready.

As my wife descended the stairwell in a white button-up blouse and navy skirt, she wore a half grin on her face. Grace walked over to join Olivia and the other sisters by the hotel entrance as Anna Beth shrugged. "I'm back to my ordinary self," she said self-consciously.

I pulled her into another embrace. "*You*, my dear, are anything but ordinary," I replied, twirling her about like we were dancing. I finished with a dip that garnered applause from the onlookers. When I lifted her up, she laughed and blushed a deep shade of pink.

"Okay, you love birds," Carrie said, motioning us toward the door. "Let's give you a proper goodbye, and then off you two go!" She handed envelopes of rice to everyone as they filed out of the hotel, and we dutifully hugged our family and friends and promised to write. Anna Beth only teared up when she bid her sisters and Grace farewell, and me, almost, when I shook Elliott's hand.

The crowd split as we hurried down the hotel steps. Everyone clapped, whistled, and tossed rice in the air. Grains of good luck showered down on us like a gentle rain, and Anna Beth squealed at my side. She covered her head as we ducked into the safety of the car, the back seat already packed with our bags. We drove away waving, tin cans rattling from our back bumper. That part was Elliott's doing... *Tin cans for my Tin Lizzie*, he had said. The thought made me chuckle.

"So, will you tell me where we're going *now*?" Anna Beth asked as we passed Carrie's house and headed up the last hill out of town.

I had purposely kept the honeymoon destination a secret, but as she reached over to tug my sleeve gently, I caved to her innocent impatience. "I'm taking you to Sanibel Island, Florida," I said. Out of the corner of my eye, I saw her jaw drop open.

"You're kidding!" she gasped. "The beach?! Are you serious?"

I nodded, not able to suppress my smile any longer. "Of course, I'm serious! I was headed to the Gulf when I stopped in Harlan. I was just going to rest a day or two and continue on, but then there you were in the post office. The rest is our beautiful history," I replied. I paused briefly, the emotion of the last months welling into a lump that stuck in my throat. After clearing it, I added, "You opened my eyes in a split second, and I knew no worldly sights could compare to seeing you for the rest of my life. So, it's fitting to take you with me to the Gulf... *and* you get to add a fifth state to your list!"

Anna Beth grinned broadly, placing her hand atop mine on the seat between us. "Thank you, Mr. Johnston," she said softly.

"You know, you can call me Daniel – I've told you that several times," I teased.

Anna Beth laughed and shrugged her shoulders, turning the conversation to the wedding and what we each had enjoyed most about the day. We eventually settled into a comfortable silence, both of us lost in separate worlds that had now collided into one.

We drove south a good piece, only getting out to walk around and use the restroom a couple of times. When night fell around us and my eyes got tired of watching the road, we stopped to rest in a small family-owned hotel. I was eager to consummate our marriage, but I knew how exhausted we both were. When I pushed through the hotel room door with our bags, seeing her curled up on the pillow fast asleep was actually a relief. *I've waited this long*, I mused, setting the bags down and changing into my pajamas, so *What is a few more nights?*

Two and a half days later, we pulled our car on the ferry to go over to Sanibel Island just before dusk. Hanging over the railing to watch the water lap against the boat, Anna Beth laughed most of the way across the bay. She confessed she had never been out on any body of water, not even on a lake in a rowboat! When we drove our car onto the island, her eyes were as big as saucers. I pointed out Bailey's Mercantile as we passed, and she motioned to the rows of houses.

"They all look the same!" she exclaimed. "I've never seen anything like it!"

"They're called Sears and Roebuck kit houses – neat, huh?" I answered, following the little winding road toward the beachfront. When I stopped in front of the unique cottage we would be calling home for a while, I relished seeing my bride's whimsical expression.

"Mr. Johnston!" she gasped, fumbling with the car's door handle to get out in a hurry. "This is the most beautiful place I have ever seen in my entire life!" She closed the car door and stood still, staring in awe at the little house and coastline beyond. I stared at her with the same genuine wonder. She was a country girl standing giddy at the edge of the world; of all the adventures I'd had, I don't think I felt any more delight.

The little yellow and white bungalow was indeed charming. It had gingerbread-style trim work in the corners of the wide front porch and was nearly glowing in the brightening moonlight as the sun fully set. What I loved most, however, was the sound of the waves and the smell of salty air. I had seen most of the seashores in America on *both* coasts, but Sanibel Island would now be my favorite.

"Just wait until you see the beach… it's right over those dunes," I said, gathering our bags from the back seat. I closed the door with my hip, and we walked to the front door. Stooping down to retrieve the key from under the mat, I added with a smile, "Welcome home."

"For how long?" she asked, her eyes shining with excitement.

"However long you want," I replied with a shrug.

She hugged my waist as I opened the front door. Anna Beth promptly made her rounds and turned on all the lights in the whole place. "They have electric lights throughout the whole house, just like a hotel!" she pointed out breathlessly.

I laughed. "Kind of – the island is powered with generators; it's a little different," I said. I hadn't told her yet, but whichever house we eventually called home for good would not only have electric lights and indoor plumbing – something else that was a treat for the more elite of society – but it would have the finest appliances money could buy.

Anna Beth explored the various rooms as I set our bags on the kitchen counter. I had asked the company that rented us this house to stock the refrigerator and cabinets before our arrival, and much to my approval, they had gone an extra step and left fresh strawberries on the counter for a sweet treat. I popped one into my mouth and savored the flavor. When Anna Beth circled the kitchen table and came back to me, I held one out to her. She ate it gingerly, not taking her eyes off mine, then wrapped her arms tightly around my waist and buried her head in my chest.

"This is more… more than…" she mumbled, struggling to find the words. "I don't…"

I lifted her chin, and when our eyes met again, I leaned down and gently kissed her. My lips wandered from her lips to her cheeks and forehead before I spoke. "Angel, I know you've had troubles and trials in this life, but this is *always* what you deserved."

Her body melted into mine as she kissed me again, her soft, warm hand wrapping around the back of my neck. I felt like someone lit a match within me, my body tingling with anticipation I had only felt twinges of since meeting her. It was a feeling I had worried I'd long outlived. Muscle memory took over as I caressed her back, my hand coming to rest in the small bend above her hips, but she suddenly pulled away with a worried expression. She placed her hand on my chest and held us apart briefly.

"I… I haven't… not since…" she began to stutter, her face flushing red. "I don't know…" I had only seen her this nervous one time, and that was at the church when she told me about her abusive past.

I nodded instantly, grasping the gravity of this moment for her, and touched my finger to her lips. "*It's okay*, Anna Beth," I spoke gently, shifting my hand to hold her chin so I could trace the outline of her lips with my thumb. "I will *never* force you to do anything you do not want to do. *Never.* You get to be in control. *Always.* You set the pace between us." I dropped my hand to her shoulder and squeezed it gently. "I'm old – I know we joke about it, but it's true. I've seen many years of life and had my fill of it. I'll follow you anywhere you lead; being with you is all that matters… and being *with* you comes with many expressions of love."

Anna Beth sighed deeply as she relaxed; it sounded like a rushing release of worry pent up for no telling how long. She drew close to me again, resting her head on my shoulder. I was content just to hold her, if that's all she wanted from me, but eventually, she lifted her face and kissed me again. Her apprehension had seemingly dissolved away, reminding me of a seagull soaring upward from the swelling tides. When she took my hand and led me down the hall, I wasn't at all surprised. I always had known my angel was stronger than her demons.

10

There is nothing like waking up next to your beloved. I might as well have died and gone to heaven. Being an early riser, I just watched her sleep peacefully until deciding to make us breakfast. When Anna Beth found her way to the kitchen about an hour later, a tender smile played on her lips.

"Good morning, Mr. Johnston," she said.

"Good morning, my angel," I answered. I was cooking eggs and bacon in a skillet, the room filling with a savory aroma. Anna Beth slipped past me and poured two glasses of juice. She slid one toward me on the counter.

"Thank you for fixing breakfast. I think I'm half starved!" she commented, rifling through the cabinets until she found dishes and silverware. I piled the food on the plates, turned off the stove, and we sat at the table by the window. She glanced at the beach, watching the waves lap gently against the shore as she took her first bite. "What do you want to do today?" she asked after swallowing.

"Whatever you would like," I replied patiently. Maybe one of these days she would fully comprehend how I was living my life for her now.

She grinned excitedly. "Can we go to the beach?"

I nodded. "That sounds like a fine plan."

We continued to talk awhile, then dressed and stepped out the sliding glass door onto the narrow back porch. There was a double swing on one end and steps leading down to the beach on the other. I motioned for her to leave her shoes by the steps, laughing at how she squealed when her bare feet touched the sand. She had never felt sand between her toes or seen the unending horizon with her own eyes; amazed by the magnificent view was a gross understatement for her. I offered my arm, and we took a long walk in the surf together. I judged it about a mile to the pier and back, pointing out crabs and clam holes along the way. She giggled like a child at Christmas to find an unbroken sand dollar.

"The shells get tossed by the sea, so people usually only find fragments," I informed her. "Sanibel Island has some of the best intact seashells, though. People come from all over to hunt them."

"Would you like to fish off the pier one day?" Anna Beth asked, shielding her eyes to watch a seagull dive for a fish in the ocean.

I wrapped my arm around her waist and squeezed. "Sure, but I don't think it'll beat fishing in the lake at Harlan," I said with a grin. The little picnic we had shared early on was one of my favorite memories. I could still see her gracefully take the little yellow flower I offered and stick it behind her ear; if I was a painter, I would have captured the image for all posterity.

We spent the next month at that lovely cottage on Sanibel Island, and I soon realized how marrying a woman a third my age was going to keep me young, whether I liked it or not! We fished off the pier several times, found many local restaurants to sample, went shopping, and saw a few of the area's attractions... but our favorite thing to do together was visit the lighthouse. It had been built in 1884 and was still in working condition. I loved to rest on a bench close by while Anna Beth alternated between staring at the giant beacon and hunting seashells – but she always came back to just admiring the lighthouse.

"What's your fascination with this place?" I called to her on one of our early evening trips. We had just watched the keeper haul the oil up the iron tower's spiral staircase and knew the light would soon come on; it was Anna Beth's favorite part.

My wife shrugged her shoulders and came to sit next to me, seashells of every kind and color filling her lap. "Oh, I don't know," she sighed contentedly. "I think I love it here because I can see a parallel between that old lighthouse bringing ships safely to shore and God shining His light out to bring me in."

My eyebrows furrowed in confusion; Anna Beth's faith was the only part of her I still couldn't work out. "How do you mean?" I questioned, honestly wanting to understand. My wife chewed her bottom lip for a moment; I could see she was mulling over how to continue, so I sat quietly waiting.

"If you think of your life being a boat on the ocean, we are all tossed to and fro from time to time," she started to explain. "My childhood – and even young adulthood – rocked me about many times; sometimes I feared I would capsize and sink! But then there was God shining His light out through the good people in my life. He shined His love so brightly that I could see my way safely to shore time and time again. I owe my life to Him. Without Him, where would my ship be?"

Our life is like a ship tossed on the ocean of circumstance; I considered the beautiful analogy. I could see myself through the years, rowing hard at times to stay afloat and at other times letting the waves carry me where they willed. *How does one make it to shore?* I pondered. That seemed like a final destination for a ship. *How can you reach it before your life is over? Isn't death the final destination of every man's life, and then – nothing?* None of it made sense, and I certainly couldn't recall any shining lights of love directing my path in life – except maybe for Anna Beth's. Maybe that is why I had made so many mistakes.

"Have *you* made it to shore already?" I asked quietly. She bobbed her head back and forth with a half grin, fingering a scalloped shell.

"Yes and no… I mean, I'll still sail the rest of my life's journey, but, in a way, I have already made it to shore because I know beyond a shadow of a doubt that God saved me and I'm going to heaven after I die," my wife confided. She dug her toes into the sand and picked them up, watching the grains slide off in every direction. "Some days I *feel* a foretaste of it even here on earth. I've never been there, but it's already home to me. I *know* I'll make it safely to the harbor and step off on the other side… and that's just about as good as already being there."

The lighthouse's beacon lit up at last, and Anna Beth gasped with delight as it flooded the area with a warm and ethereal glow. I slipped my arm around her shoulders and squeezed gently. We both stared out at the ocean, trying to see how far the light could reach before it faded into darkness. Without another word, we eventually clasped hands and walked home along the beach, her other hand holding her dress hem up in a makeshift pocket for the shells while the surf lapped our ankles. I didn't want to continue our conversation, and she seemed to sense my need for solitude. The concept of life after death was so foreign to me; even in war, I hadn't wrapped my mind around the possibility. I just assumed when I died, everything was over. I felt exhausted at the idea of there being more. However, I knew one thing for certain – I wasn't going to get the wondering out of my mind any time soon. Anna Beth was so certain there was a heaven, and she was going there. My heart ached with the longing to join her in this wonderful forever....

After the fifth week of our honeymoon, every day just as good as the last, I found Anna Beth sitting on the porch swing out back. She had disappeared a while before, and I had missed her. I paused at the screen door, watching her stare out at the quiet, rhythmic waves as the sun drooped low, lighting the sky every shade of red, pink, and orange. I could tell her mind was a million miles away, and I wondered where exactly. Finally, I cleared my throat, startling her back to reality.

"Sorry to bother you, Angel. You can stay out as long as you like. Do you need anything?" I inquired quietly. She smiled softly and patted the swing next to her, inviting me to join.

"Mr. Johnston?" she asked, leaning her head on my shoulder while simultaneously pulling her legs up under her. I had told her to call me Daniel a million times, but she insisted that my formal name showed the respect I deserved.

"Yes?" I answered, resting my hand on her knee.

"*Where* is our home going to be? Is it back in Harlan? Tennessee? One of the other states you've visited?" she wondered. I breathed a little easier; she was just getting tired of the beach, not me.

"You're ready to leave?" I replied.

She sat up and ran her hand through her hair. "I've loved *every* minute, but yes. I'm imagining the life we're going to build together once we settle somewhere! Before our whirlwind marriage, you were living in a hotel and I in my best friend's house...." She chuckled at the thought and then grew serious again. "So, I've just been thinking: where will *our* home be? Have you thought about it?"

I shrugged my shoulders and spoke honestly. "I've been everywhere and seen everything. I'm truly okay settling anywhere you like. Did you decide if you wanted to pursue teaching again?" I asked. Anna Beth sighed deeply, looking back at the ocean.

"Teaching was the hardest two years of my life," she admitted. "It was the most rewarding, too, of course. I know I made a difference... but it took every ounce of me, you know what I mean?" My wife looked at me with conflicted feelings dancing in her eyes. "I feel guilty for not wanting to go back to the profession, but I really just want to enjoy being your wife right now. It's like life has finally fallen into place for me."

I wrapped my arm around her shoulders, and she snuggled into my chest as the ocean air became chilly with sunset. "Guilt is a funny thing. I think we all feel driven to be more and do more – it's human nature. I also think it is okay to settle into what makes you feel good inside, too, though. I'll support you in anything you want to do. You know I have more than enough money to take care of us, but if teaching is something you *must* do, then do it."

Anna Beth sat quietly for several minutes as we swung, both of us listening to the waves crash upon the seashore in the darkness. "I thought about going back to Missouri," she eventually offered, "but I hate to be so far from Grace and Olivia, and the thought of Missouri still makes me powerfully homesick at times... I still want to know what happened to my parents. I think if we moved to Missouri, the questions would consume me again." She tucked a loose lock of hair behind her ear.

I knew the mystery of her parents' disappearance still weighed on her after all these years, even though she worked so hard to rise above it. Before Mr. Jingle passed, he had continued the search by writing letters and calling various towns... but nothing ever turned up. It was like they had just *vanished*. The thoughts of leaving my own children, and how I *should* let them know I was alive and still loved them after all these years, pressed into my mind once again. I cleared my throat. *They've grown up now, and I don't have a right to intrude on their lives; they wouldn't want to be a part of my and Anna Beth's new life anyway – if I couldn't make it work with their own mother,* I told myself.

"It sounds like Missouri is out then. We can go to Tennessee instead," I suggested. She considered the possibility and then crossed her arms doubtfully.

"But I like being close to Carrie, *too*," she replied with a laugh. "I know I'm being impossible; forgive me!"

I leaned in and kissed the top of her head. "There's nothing to forgive. The whole world is yours to choose from, and I'll always love Harlan because that is where we met. I have heard, however, that the coal strikes are only getting worse around those parts," I said. "Someone was killed just the other day. I'm afraid if it keeps escalating, the town'll soon be crawling with soldiers. There's no knowing how long it'll take to settle the matter." I didn't explain the rest of my reasoning for not considering moving to Harlan permanently, but the mere appearance of war-like conditions, along with it being the place where Anna Beth was attacked, dredged up too many memories we both respectively were working to repress.

"Well, there was always this other part of Kentucky my Daddy talked about before our move to Harlan called Edmonson County. He said the Green River runs through it, and, along with the coal mines, there were caves to explore," she recalled, genuinely smiling as she thought back on it. "When I was a girl... I don't know, I daydreamed about it. He made it sound so wonderful and intriguing!"

"I've been through Kentucky several times, but I've never been to Edmonson County," I said, nodding approvingly. "I know where about it is, though. It's west of Harlan, so an easy trip to see Carrie but not too far from Grace and Olivia in Tennessee."

"You mean *I* thought of a place *you've* never been?" Anna Beth sat up and grinned proudly at me. I couldn't help but laugh.

"Seems you did! It sounds like a nice place to call home – would you like to give it a go?" I asked, drawing little circles on her knee with my thumb. She leaned over and kissed my cheek.

"I think that's a great idea," she said. "Thank you, Mr. Johnston... for *everything*."

I cupped her knee and squeezed, my voice choking with emotion. "Don't you know by now?" I asked sincerely. "You *are* my everything."

11

We left for Edmonson County, Kentucky, at the end of the week and rented a room at the Reed Hotel when we pulled into Brownsville. It had similar features to the Michaels' Hotel in Harlan, and I could tell that made Anna Beth feel more comfortable... which also helped me relax. I was used to bouncing around from place to place, but she had only moved – and started over – a handful of times; to say she was a bundle of nerves was an understatement.

The next day, Anna Beth went out exploring the town while I started negotiations with a real estate agent to find us a home. He showed us several different houses and plots over the next couple of weeks, and I was relieved when Anna Beth fell in love with a piece of land a few miles north of Brownsville. It was close to a little stream that ribboned through the base of a holler, its dips and ridges giving way to woods on the far side. I wouldn't have swayed her opinion for anything as I wanted her to have everything she dreamed of, but that property struck my fancy as well! I bought the land outright, hired a construction crew to build a large farmhouse in the clearing, and in a few short months, we were settling into our new home – the one we built together.

The farmhouse was painted light blue with white shutters, and it had a wide porch all the way across the front. We also splurged for the asphalt roofing shingles that had recently come to market. Among the six rooms, we had our own kitchen – large enough for a full table, sitting room with a fireplace, bathroom, and bedroom, with two more rooms upstairs... all of which had electric lights, indoor plumbing, and the best appliances money could buy. I found my wife holding on to the kitchen sink one day in complete awe, and she told me how when she was a girl, they had to fill a wash bin with water from the pump, set it on the counter, and wash their hands and dishes in it. *My own sink with running water!* she had said with wonder, running her hands along the rim and faucet.

She invited Carrie to visit as soon as she was able, and I chuckled to see the two of them jump into each other's arms when she arrived. Anna Beth took half a day showing her around the house and land while I enjoyed a much-needed break, piddling around with my tools in the barn we also had built.

"You have a *phonograph*?" Carrie had asked one evening while we were sitting around the fireplace. She stared at the recording machine and its basket of tinfoil coated cylinders in the corner of the room.

"Yes! Isn't it neat? Do you want to record your voice?" Anna Beth answered, rising from her rocking chair. She set it up, turned the handle, and nodded to her friend to start talking.

"Anna Beth Atwood Johnston," Carrie leaned forward and spoke into the phonograph, "you are the *luckiest* woman in Kentucky – no, America – no! the world!" They both laughed while Anna Beth switched the needles and played the words back several times.

For two weeks, Carrie and Anna Beth fixed meals together, cleaned house, went into town to shop, and played records on the Victrola. I think their favorite part, though, was sitting on the porch, staying up to all hours of the night talking.

One night while I lay in bed, listening to their laughter drift up from the porch and in through our open bedroom window, I thought again how *I* was the lucky one in this arrangement. My parents' farmhouse in Oregon, where Clara and some of the kids may still be for all I knew, swam into my consciousness. I had dreamed of filling that house with love and family and had come close, but my former life paled in comparison to my Kentucky home with Anna Beth. *I might be too old to fill this house with family, but it would see plenty of love,* I mused. I had wandered all over the United States looking for a place that I could call my own; I had bought several different houses just to turn around, sell them again, and move on to the next best thing. I closed my eyes and breathed deeply, bringing my thoughts back to the cozy bedroom. I would never sell this house nor move on until I died and left this world all together. I had finally found a place to call *home*, and it was absolute perfection in my eyes.

The only real challenge we had faced thus far was that Anna Beth and I were attempting to get to know our neighbors as we frequented the mercantile and shops in town. People assumed she was my granddaughter, which made us both chuckle like our age difference was a private joke. Naturally, when they found out we were *married*, we had to wait for them to get over their shock, put their judgements aside, and get to know us as a couple! Most people hastily excused themselves because they didn't know what to say and just avoided us from that point on. Some continued to look at us warily or worst, in disgust. The ones who managed to accept the unconventionality of our relationship, however, grew to call us good friends. That is how we came to know James and Rose Mutter.

I remembered the day we went to the mercantile for a few groceries and this middle-aged couple walked up to us in the fruits and vegetables aisle. They introduced themselves, agreeing it was nice to see new faces in Edmonson County, and said they had been meaning to welcome us to town.

"Are ya an' y'grandfather jus' passin' through?" Rose had asked Anna Beth.

My wife smiled and introduced herself and me as her *husband*, also offering that we had built a house down in the holler as a quick change of subject. Everyone knew the holler where the river ran through the bluffs, so that at least was common ground for easy conversation after such a shock. The Mutters' faces registered the surprise we were accustomed to, but they recovered themselves in record time... and best of all, they didn't turn and walk away! James actually grinned and shook my hand.

"*Well*, Mr. Johnston – I'm not sure where yer from or what they put in y'water, but I sure do want some!" he had said. Rose gasped and hit her husband on the arm with her purse, but he just laughed louder. Anna Beth and I laughed, too, and eventually Rose joined in, red cheeks and all. The interaction instantly reminded me of Elliott and Carrie, which was refreshing and comforting all at the same time. The Mutters invited us to supper that very night, and we graciously accepted. It was our first home invitation since we had arrived several months before, and it felt good to expand the joyful bubble we had been living in to include new friends.

The Mutters were wonderful people, too. Both in their early fifties, they were just the right age to connect with Anna Beth yet still relate to me. I think Anna Beth appreciated them most because they introduced her to the church community in town; James was a deacon at Still Valley, which evidently was of the same faith and order as the childhood churches. Since she was a God-fearing woman, I knew she had been missing going to church something awful... but what touched *me* was that she never made me feel guilty for not attending with her every Sunday.

My wife knew I would go anywhere to please her, but she also realized organized religion wasn't quite my cup of tea. I wasn't much for sitting on a hard pew with a few dozen other folk, listening to a man preach at me; it sounded like a bunch of hollering more than anything! I'd much rather take solitary Sunday walks through the woods by our stream and appreciate God in the nature all around me. That being said, however, I did attend special services like Christmas and Easter with my wife. I knew it meant the world to her, and her hug and kiss afterward was enough to make the hour and a half inside the church house bearable.

A year or so passed since our move to Edmonson County, and we were hosting the Mutters for supper. They had frequented our home enough that Rose walked straight in without knocking, immediately admiring the new Imperial ripple vase on the sideboard near the fireplace. The delicate glass had a scalloped edge and fluted feet with rich, swirling colors, and it was filled with the white and pink flowers from the fields.

"Anna Beth Johnston!" she exclaimed. "Where in the world did y'find such a treasure? I simply *love* it! I ain't seen anythin' like it at the mercantile..."

"Thanks, Rose," Anna Beth replied sincerely. She walked over and ran her finger along the vase's rim. "It's called Carnival Glass. Mr. Johnston got it from a mail order business, the *Lee's Catalogue*, for our first anniversary."

Rose's jaw dropped open. "*Honey*, that magazine is the envy of ev'ry housewife ev'rywhere! From practical necessities t'fashionable decoratin' n'lifestyle..." she quoted bits of the magazine's advertisement as her voice trailed off dreamily.

James patted his wife on the back. "Now, Rose, y'ain't covetin', are ya?" he teased. Spending time with a church deacon and his wife had taught me a few things, like how not coveting was one of the Ten

Commandments in the Bible; therefore, I understood the joke and chuckled.

"Of course not, y'old coot!" Rose fussed while smacking her husband's arm away. He backed up from her with a cackle that had both Anna Beth and me laughing out loud before their skirmish was over.

"Alright, I think it's about time for supper!" Anna Beth suggested, a smile still gracing her face.

We gathered in the dining room where she served fried chicken, green beans, and hash brown casserole. My wife never served corn, which our friends didn't seem to notice. Corn reminded her of the Graingers' farm where she spent those few troublesome years. I wasn't sure how much of her past she had confided in Rose, but I never mentioned it. It wasn't my place to stir up old feelings when Anna Beth was seemingly past all of it and happy with how her life turned out. That's why I just winked at her as she gave me a second helping of green beans.

"That was simply delicious, Anna Beth," Rose complimented, dabbing her mouth with a napkin. She rose to help Anna Beth clear the supper plates and serve the chocolate cake. "Jus' *look* at y'new dessert plates! Are these from *Lee's Catalogue*, too?" She held up a cream-colored plate with a floral pattern for her husband to see.

"Rose...," James said warningly. She rolled her eyes, putting the plate down, and we all laughed. When the women sat back down at the table to eat their cake, however, Anna Beth suddenly looked dazed.

I noticed her sway sideways in the chair and put both her hands on the table to steady herself. Concerned, I stood half up and reached for her arm. "Are you all right, Angel?" I asked.

My wife glanced my way and nodded slowly, swallowing intentionally. "Yes, I just felt a little woozy all of a sudden...," she replied. With a look around at our worried friends, she forced a smile and added, "I'm sorry, everyone! You all enjoy dessert – I think I'll step outside for a breath of fresh air."

James and I rose as Anna Beth stood up, and Rose said, "I'll go with ya, honey." We watched the women exit the room before sitting back down together, our eyebrows raised in unison.

"I wonder what got inta y'wife?" James asked, picking his fork back up to dig into his cake slice. "Has she been feelin' ill lately?"

"Not that I know of," I replied with a shrug of my shoulders. My concern lessened now that I knew Rose was tending to her; she had a way of getting to the bottom of things and would tell me if anything was wrong. "She's been a bit tired lately, and the kitchen does stay warm after all the cooking and baking," I offered as a possible explanation. James shifted the conversation to the radio news and impending fall weather as we ate our dessert, but when the ladies *still* hadn't come back after a half an hour, he stood and stretched.

"It's prob'ly time fo' us t'be headin' out," James said, reaching to shake my hand. "Thank y'fo havin' us in y'home 'gain." I accompanied him to the front porch; it was already getting dark outside, but the one overhead light gave off a soft glow that bugs buzzed around.

Rose glanced our way as the door creaked open and hushed whatever she had been saying. "I'll talk t'ya *real* soon, sweetheart," she said instead, tenderly hugging Anna Beth.

"Are y'feelin' better?" James inquired, offering his arm to his wife as they prepared to walk down the steps to their car.

"Yes, much," Anna Beth replied, leaning against one of the porch posts. She briefly looked in my direction but averted her eyes while waving good-bye to our friends. "You all be careful going home, okay?" she called out. James and Rose nodded as they climbed into their car. My concern rebounded at Anna Beth's anxious look. *Was she ill? Was she upset with me for some reason?* I worried.

I cleared my throat and hollered farewell to the Mutters as their car engine rumbled to life and they pulled out our dirt driveway. James waved his hand out the open window while Rose craned her neck to look back at Anna Beth. I thought I glimpsed a smile on her lips, but it was too dark to discern the expression exactly. *What was going on here?* I contemplated.

As our friends drove out of sight, I walked to my wife and slipped my arms around her from behind. The fireflies were just starting to glitter the night with their soft, glowing lights, and we both watched them for a few minutes without speaking. When Anna Beth finally relaxed against me, the back of her head resting on my shoulder, I couldn't stand the silence any longer.

"What's wrong, Angel?" I asked quietly. "Are you sick... or upset..."

Anna Beth placed her hands on mine, our fingers interlocking atop her stomach, and took a deep breath. "You're *partly* right," she said, "about the sick part." My mind began to race; *I* always expected to be the sick or feeble one – not her!

"Do you need a doctor?" I pressed quickly.

"Not yet," she replied, her voice teasingly lilting upward. I gently turned her around to face me and saw a little smirk inch up her face.

"You need to tell me what's wrong right *now*," I said sternly, tired of the confusing charade. Anna Beth shrugged her shoulders and wrapped her arms around my waist.

"You can call a doctor in about six months," she offered nonchalantly. When she noted my persistent ignorance, she chuckled and gave me a quick kiss. "*Mr. Johnston – I'm with child!*" she finally exclaimed. "Rose thinks I'm maybe three or four months along. You're going to be a father... again."

All reasoning ground to a halt; I must not have heard her right. *She was with child? Is that what she had said?* I backtracked. *Rose would know; she had raised six children that were all Anna Beth's age or older now.* Anna Beth stood quietly with a smile on her face, allowing the idea to slowly seep into me and take root as it had her.

"You're – we're – having a child? *Us?*" I asked, still dumbfounded. "Anna Beth, are you *sure*? I didn't think..."

She nodded and kissed me again, intentionally and with more feeling. "Yes, I understand it now," she said when we pulled apart. "It's the same fluttering feeling, the same nauseousness I experienced when I was...." Her voice trailed off, and I knew she was thinking of the short time she had carried Mr. Grainger's baby before the beating and miscarriage. After a short pause, my wife looked up at me again, her eyes brimming with tears. "I wasn't sure if I even *wanted* to be pregnant again, not after the last experience and all, but now that I am, I'm so... *happy*. Are you happy?"

"Yes," I choked out quickly. "Of course, I am!" Tears welled up in my own eyes, and we cried together there on the front porch of our farmhouse, on our plot of land with the gentle stream that ran through the holler, our arms locked around one another for the longest time.

Another child... our child! I considered the impossible miracle. Our marriage was enough of a marvel, but this was something we didn't even know to hope for. Standing there, I thought of two trees that had grown from different roots, their branches intertwining through the mercy of time, and I just held on to my beloved wife. I had let go of my first family, a mistake that somehow led to such an amazing blessing, but I didn't ever want to let go of Anna Beth or this new child. I promised myself right then and there that I would be better this time around, and I meant it with every fiber of my being.

12

Anna Beth's stomach swelled exponentially in the following months. At first it was just a slight bump under her blouse, but it quickly grew into a perfectly round ball. I bought a telephone for the house so she could talk to her sisters, Grace, and Carrie without walking to the store, and Rose started visiting more often as well – often with an entourage! She and the church women were accomplished seamstresses, and while I could have bought Anna Beth all new clothes to accommodate her growing shape, she was most content to sit among the ladies as they brought their quilting circles to our home and let out the waistlines of her favorite skirts. They also made several patchwork quilts for the baby, which, being born in the heart of winter, would be greatly appreciated.

I considered using the telephone to tell Elliott our unbelievably good news but decided to pen it down as usual. Something this special needed to be told with care and effort. That's why one Sunday morning when Anna Beth had gone to church with the Mutters – they had taken to picking her up so she didn't have to walk both ways in her condition – I settled at the desk in the corner of our upper bedroom and pulled out a piece of paper and my favorite ink pen. After collecting my thoughts, I wrote:

Dear Elliott,

I hope this letter finds you well. I could have called, but we've written letters all our lives and this just feels right. You will never believe the news I have to tell you this time – Anna Beth is with child! I don't know how... well, of course, I know how... but isn't it incredible?

We think the baby will come mid to late winter. We saw a doctor in town, and he said mother and baby are the picture of health! He also said that while it is unusual to father children at my age, it isn't unheard of. I'm speechless. She not only marries me but now gives me a child in my old age? I love her more every day if that is possible.

Come for a visit any time; we'd love to see you again. You can just show up on our doorstep unannounced, okay? You are always welcome in our home. Take care of yourself, my friend.

Sincerely,
Daniel

I carefully folded the letter, slid it into an envelope, and tucked it into my breast pocket before making my way down to the stream that led the way to town. Absent mindedly following its winding banks, I loved hearing the crisp fall leaves crunch beneath my boots. Autumn was in full swing, and the trees had turned brilliant shades of yellow, orange, red, and burnt umber. I tilted my head back and breathed in the refreshing, cool breeze as I meandered along. A fox family darting in and out of their den beneath a bluff caught my eye, along with a woodpecker who was tapping out a repetitive rhythm in the distance. I smiled to myself.

My mind wandered to the God Anna Beth talked about so often; as I looked around at my surroundings, I contemplated, *Surely, there is a God.* Only God of heaven and earth could pattern such nature in its perfection and breathe life back into an old man in the form of a loving wife and family! *What had I done to deserve such mercy and grace?* The question still baffled me. I knew better than anyone how terribly unworthy I was. I had left my first family, been a railing drunkard at times, and became a vagabond without any purpose at all. *Why would God bless me with a second chance at happiness?* My thoughts shifted back to my beautiful and deserving wife... maybe I had found favor by default. Anna Beth was probably one of His favorite angels, too.

Once in town, I left my letter in the out-going post box and glanced at my watch. It was nearing one o'clock in the afternoon; church would let out any moment. I walked through town to catch Anna Beth, thinking if we took our time, perhaps she would fancy a walk home through the woods. As I neared the building, however, Anna Beth caught the first glimpse of me and was instantly alarmed.

"Mr. Johnston!" she called with a wave, breaking apart from Rose and a few other women to rush to my side. "Is everything okay? Why are you in town?" Her unwavering love and concern made me smile, as did her soft, milky skin, rosy cheeks, and golden-brown hair shining in the sun. I didn't know how she could grow to be any more beautiful but being with child had somehow enhanced every lovely feature!

"Yes, hon," I answered quickly, resting my hands on her shoulders to settle the matter. "I was just dropping a letter off for Elliott. It's a beautiful day for a walk, don't you think?"

James and Rose made their way over to us, and I shook my friend's hand. "Nice t'see ya, Daniel! How're ya t'day?" he asked, a big grin on his face.

"Doing just fine, kind sir," I replied with a wink.

"Would y'all like t'join Rose n'me fo' supper?" he inquired.

"I appreciate the invitation, James, but I was going to see if Anna Beth wanted to walk home this afternoon," I suggested. "At your pace of course, my dear," I added to my wife, who was rubbing her round stomach gently. She looked down the road toward the stream that disappeared into the woods and smiled at the thought.

"We can take y'both home in the car if y'don't feel like walkin', dear," Rose offered, eyeing Anna Beth carefully. "Y'don't want t'overdo it..."

"I wouldn't mind the walk, Rose. Thank you, though," Anna Beth replied, looking back at our friends. She wrapped her arm through mine and gently squeezed. "I might *feel* enormous, but I'm not so big I can't make it home on my own just yet!" she laughed.

Clasping hands, we bid our friends good-bye and ambled toward the well-trodden path that led back to our farmhouse. Anna Beth breathed in the fresh air as I had done earlier and nudged me with her hip.

"This was a lovely surprise," she noted warmly.

"I thought so. I enjoyed the walk here so much, I figured you may enjoy the walk home," I replied, wrapping my arm around her waist.

"Did you tell Elliott about the baby?" she asked. I nodded excitedly.

"I bet he falls out of his chair when he reads it! I hope he doesn't break a hip," I said with a grin. The idea caught Anna Beth off guard, and she giggled.

As we wove our way deeper into the woods, water dashed through the creek bed alongside us, flowing around rocks that created little dips and waterspouts in the current. The rushing sound added to the calm feeling of a leisurely Sunday stroll.

"I reckon I have two or three more months," Anna Beth said after a few minutes of silence. "I think it's time we discuss baby names, don't you?" She reached out and snapped a twig off a nearby tree as she passed, twirling the shoot in her fingers. "Do you have any favorites?" Her interest took me by surprise; I hadn't yet considered baby names.

I shrugged my shoulders. "Not really. You?" I countered. She shook her head.

"I just don't know… I think it's kind of hard to name someone you've not seen," she confided, tossing the twig into the stream and resting her hands atop her stomach.

"Why don't we wait until the babe is born then?" I suggested. "Then we can get a good look at the child and decide something fitting."

Anna Beth halted suddenly and reached for my hand, placing it firmly on her stomach. I stopped walking and felt a poke under my palm. With a laugh, I brought both hands to the spot, hoping to feel it again. After a moment of stillness, I gently pushed on her belly and the baby pushed against my hands again.

"He or she is awfully feisty today!" I exclaimed, beaming at my wife. She laughed as we finished our game of poke.

"I think he or she fancies long walks in the woods with Papa," she said, tucking a strand of hair behind her ear as we started back toward the house. I liked the sound of that, and she knew it. *Papa.* I held the blessing deep within my heart.

In the weeks to come, winter blew in with a vengeance, and a significant snow fell right after Christmas. We had fireplaces in both our upstairs bedroom and downstairs living room, and, thankfully, James had helped me split plenty of firewood as my joints ached more with the cold weather these days than ever before. I stoked a warm fire all day and night, and Anna Beth took to staying in our bedroom to both be near the heat and to avoid the stairs. She was growing increasingly uncomfortable as January crept in. I waited on her hand and foot, her smile lighting up the room when I carried in our mail-ordered crib. I had tucked one of the church ladies' little quilts inside it and placed the tiny wooden piece right next to Anna Beth's side of the bed. Her excitement was contagious as she thanked me a hundred times over for making her a mother. It wasn't too many days later when she beckoned me upstairs and said the much-anticipated words through clenched teeth: *It's time.*

I rushed downstairs to telephone James; we all knew the plan! He and Rose would pick up the doctor and come right over. They only lived ten minutes away by car, but time seemed to stand still while I paced the living room, stopping occasionally to peer out the front door. I had never been happier to see Rose bustle up the front steps, laden with clean linen and a pot for hot water.

"We have plenty of supplies here, Rose," I said after throwing open the door for her. She pushed past me and started up the stairs, not even breaking her stride.

"Mr. Johnston," she called over her shoulder, "these towels n'this here pot have helped birth over a dozen babies in Edmonson County! Y'stay down here with James now n'let the doc n'me do what we know bes'.". Where some men could have been offended by her superior tone, I only felt a rush of relief. I was more than thankful Rose was here to support Anna Beth in Grace's stead.

The men hurried inside, the doctor heading upstairs with his bag and James making himself at home by the fireplace. He lit a pipe and handed it to me as I joined him. Anna Beth moaned loudly upstairs and then cut loose with a scream that startled us both; I had almost forgotten the pains of childbirth as I wasn't even allowed in the house when Clara was in labor. James shook his head and laughed while patting my arm.

"Even after six o'm'own, that sound still catches me by su'prise! Keep puffin', old friend – it'll calm the nerves," he advised, his eyes twinkling with excitement.

James was a good friend to have around at a time like this; he continually changed the subject of our conversation to keep me distracted, and when my pipe ran out, he offered to refill it several times. Eventually, however, I stood and started to pace again. Anna Beth's moaning and crying overhead sounded so excruciating, I was sure I'd be in the grave by the time the baby came. I wanted to sprint up the stairs and take the pain from her, knowing very well I couldn't do either of those things! I covered my face in my hands and let my thin fingers slide down my cheeks; the feeling of utter helplessness was draining my energy fast.

When the screaming mounted to a rhythmic rise and fall, James stood and laid a firm hand on my shoulder. "It's not long now," he said quietly. We both held our breath and listened, releasing a sigh of relief only when Anna Beth's cries subsided and we heard the faintest cry of a babe. James laughed and hugged me tightly, slapping my back in congratulation.

"There y'have it, Daniel! Y'child's come into this world at last!" James said with a grin. He checked his watch. "One fifty-eight in the mornin'. My goodness, that baby kep' us all up pas' bedtime!"

My heart leapt in my chest as that feeble cry grew into a wail. I could remember the cries of my other children, and the memories mixing with the present joy started me laughing, too. *I'm a father again, and this child will really know their Papa – I'll make sure of it this time!* I determined. As quickly as the elation came, worry crept in around the edges; I hadn't heard Anna Beth's voice since the baby was born. I headed up the stairs with James right on my heels.

We rounded the corner toward the bedroom just as Rose opened the door. She and I were both a sight. I was panting to catch my breath, and her brown curls stuck to her red, sweaty face. Her eyes, however, were dancing with delight. James gripped my shoulders from behind as we awaited her news.

"Ev'ryone is jus' fine, Mr. Johnston! Y'should b'*very* proud o'y'wife… come n'meet y' baby girl," she announced, wiping her hands on a towel. I peered over top of her and saw Anna Beth holding a bundle of blankets, the doctor's stethoscope shoved deep inside the folds. They all smiled as I entered the room.

"A girl?" I echoed. Rose took me by the elbow and guided me toward the bed; it felt like I was floating. She smoothed Anna Beth's hair from her face with a tender touch.

My wife looked up at me, exhausted but well pleased. "Isn't she *lovely*?" she whispered, tilting her arms toward me. I caught my first glimpse of a little round head; my daughter's tiny face was scrunched into a sleepy frown, her eyes closed as she sucked on two fingers. She had Anna Beth's nose and mouth for sure. *My little angel*, I thought to myself, and the perfect name came to me.

"*Joy*," I whispered to my wife. "Let's call her Joy."

Anna Beth stared at the baby in her arms and beamed. "I love that name! What about Joy Elizabeth – after your mother?" I laughed and wiped a tear from my eye, the breath catching in my throat. It couldn't be more ideal. "Would you like to hold her?" Anna Beth asked, holding the baby up enough for me to slip my arms around her.

It had been a long time since I last held an infant. Joy Elizabeth felt like a fragile egg cuddled against my chest. She was so small, so *young*! She was just starting out in this life whereas I was on my way out. We were two worlds barely brushing each other's edges in time and space. Tears continued to leak from my eyes. No doubt she would see and experience things I never would. It saddened me to think I'd leave her here without a Papa all too soon, but it also brought me great happiness to think a piece of my and Anna Beth's rare love would carry on.

"You know," Anna Beth said through her own tears, "I always wondered if I could have loved my first baby – the one I lost – as much as another that was mine by choice…." She reached out her hand and rested it gently atop mine. "I could have."

The doctor cleared his throat. "Mother and baby need to rest now," he spoke quietly, patting my arm on his way out the door. "It was a long delivery, but they both did well. You've got a good, strong woman, Mr. Johnston."

"Yes, I do," I replied, handing Joy back to her mother. "That, I've always known." I leaned down to kiss my wife, lingering with my lips pressed against her warm forehead. Everything I loved about this world had just doubled.

James took the doctor home, and Rose stayed with us for the next week. She tended to our every need and helped Anna Beth in ways I never would have thought of. Then she organized the church women to stop by in shifts to drop off meals and take care of the women's work around the house. They were like an army of ants marching in and out, leaving the place spotless and supper on the table in their wake! I profusely thanked each one of them and spent my time keeping the fires lit, the house warm, and visiting my wife and child in the bedroom. Anna Beth also had me call or write everyone she could think to announce the birth of our new little bundle, Joy.

One afternoon, I walked into the bedroom to find my wife standing by the window. "I think I'm ready to come downstairs," she said. "I would love to sit in the kitchen for a meal. Can you bring Joy down?" I knew there was no sense in arguing with her when she had decided something, so I picked up my daughter from the crib and followed Anna Beth to the steps.

"Hold the rail," I cautioned, "and watch your step..."

She glanced over her shoulder at me with a mischievous grin. "Yes, *Papa*," she teased.

"And look where you're going," I added. She laughed heartily, the sound filling the house and startling the babe in my arms.

At seventy-seven, I took my advice just as seriously. I slowly made my way down the steps behind my wife, cradling Joy Elizabeth in the crook of one arm while holding the rail tightly with the other hand. When we all reached the bottom, I sighed in relief and handed Joy back to her mother.

Winter quickly melted into spring and the birds and wildlife came out from their hiding places. Nature's delightful music filled the days, and our little family of three spent a lot of time on the porch swinging, rocking, talking, and laughing – even Joy was beginning to grin and giggle in little spurts. Anna Beth and I would hand the baby back and forth to each other, my wife stepping inside to nurse our daughter until she was milk-drunk and cooing, then I would get the immense pleasure of rocking her to sleep on my chest with a full belly.

"Did you rock your other children to sleep?" Anna Beth asked me out of the blue one day. We were enjoying the warm afternoon breeze, she on the porch swing and I in a rocking chair nearby. She hadn't asked about my first family in quite a while, and the question caught me by surprise.

"Occasionally," I murmured, gazing down at Joy. "Why do you ask?"

"You just look mesmerized by her all the time, so I wondered how involved you were with your other children," she explained, shrugging her shoulders as she relaxed back onto the swing.

I rocked a few more beats. My newest daughter had already doubled in weight and was growing longer every day; with her head tucked under my chin, her toes nearly reached my waist. Sleeping peacefully, she made little puffing sounds as she breathed out. She also had hold of my finger with her delicate hand. I compared this feeling to those with my other children, sifting through the experiences like mining for bits of gold among a panful of sand and rock.

"I wasn't as involved as I wanted to be, and honestly, I wasn't always in good enough shape to *be* involved – especially after the war. Clara had a maid, though, and between the two of them, they did everything for the children," I remembered aloud. "Most of the time, I just felt like I was taking up space, so eventually, I stopped trying to press myself into their lives. I'm not sure if the last couple were even my children... but I still think of them as mine."

Anna Beth sat quietly, watching a squirrel uncover its winter stash of nuts across the yard. He stuffed several morsels into his cheeks and ran up a nearby tree. "I can't imagine how your wife felt, losing you to the war and then not knowing how to reconnect after what you both undoubtedly went through," she finally replied, "but I can tell you this, Mr. Johnston – that there is your child, and I want you involved in her life as much as you can be." She had a knack for knowing the right things to say at the right times, and her words settled deep inside me; it was another thing I loved about her. "I'm sure your other children would want to know what happened to you, too," she added. "It may be painful, but it could also be a great gift for all of you."

"I'll think about it," I said sincerely. "Do you know I love you, Anna Beth Johnston?"

She smiled that angel smile, the one she and Joy now shared, and whispered back, "And I, *you*, Mr. Johnston, with all my heart."

13

Joy Elizabeth grew alongside the spring flowers, and Anna Beth's proudest day was when she dressed her all in white, complete with a little lacy bonnet that matched her dress, and took her to church for the first time. Since it was Easter Sunday, I joined them for the special service, knowing it meant the world to my wife that I was in attendance. Countless faces swirled around us, most with heartfelt congratulations and a few obviously just curious. Even though I wasn't much of a church goer, myself, I had to admit this church's parishioners were some of the kindest folks in town; their sense of community was unrivaled by anything I had ever experienced. I'd never forget how they rallied together to care for us in those early days after Joy's birth, especially since they hadn't known us long and didn't owe us a thing!

Marrying Anna Beth and having Joy made me think about a lot of new things, but this particular experience started me contemplating the true meaning of Christian charity. *Could it be that I had lived most of my life – with all the things I had seen and done – and had missed the point of it all?* I often wondered. I didn't allow myself to dwell on these kinds of thoughts too long, however; they were beginning to unsettle me. I tried instead to focus solely on the happiness I had left... surely that was enough.

The summer and fall passed swiftly, and around Christmas, Grace and Olivia came to visit. Anna Beth was over the moon to see them again as we hadn't been together since the wedding, and she cried when they brought in an old, beat-up writing desk they said had been her father's.

"Mr. Johnston! Isn't it wonderful?" my wife exclaimed, jumping up and down with giddiness. "Grace and Mr. Jingle tracked it down a few years back and gave it to me; they said they'd hold it at their house until I got a home of my own! It's such a lovely piece of my parents and our life before Harlan..." she mused as Grace and I moved it into the corner by the fireplace.

Joy, an almost one-year-old babe now, crawled to the new piece of furniture and pulled herself up with a giggle. Olivia reached down and swung her niece into the air, both laughing at the fun, and for the rest of their visit, the two were inseparable. I tried to keep myself busy during the days to allow the women uninterrupted time together, but at night I greatly enjoyed joining them around the fire. One evening, I quietly listened as their conversation shifted to telling stories of their time together in Harlan. Anna Beth told me how Grace used to help her wrap her feet with strips of fabric in the winter so her toes wouldn't get frostbit inside her old pair of too-big boots. She was laughing about it now although I'm sure it was no laughing matter when she was young, alone, and scared.

"I was appreciative, Grace, don't get me wrong... but the rags didn't help much!" Anna Beth was saying. Even though her eyes were red from lack of sleep – she and Olivia had taken to spending late nights on the front porch – I grinned, happy she was enjoying her time with her family so robustly. "Remember how we had to set the boots by the fire at night to dry them out for the next day?" she asked.

"They were an old pair o'm'ex-husband's boots," Grace replied, nodding in recognition. "One shoe had a hole in it, n'I tried t'stitch it shut. It jus' wasn't much use! Mr. Grainger wouldn't allow me t'buy ya a new pair, y'know." She grew quiet as she recalled the memory herself; it was obviously tainted with more darkness than Anna Beth's by the hint of sadness swirling in her eyes. "I wish I had been brave n'bought ya a new pair anyway," she added regretfully.

Anna Beth's contentment melted away as she shook her head. I knew the conversation was about to take a turn into dangerous territory; Anna Beth had told me they rarely spoke of the man who burdened them so. Even I knew enough of their story to know if Grace had gone against her husband's wishes, he would have beaten her for it.

"Boots were not something to start a fight about," my wife insisted, laying a gentle hand on Grace's arm. "We turned out just fine without a new pair of boots, don't you think?"

The room fell quiet, and I thought of how Anna Beth had finally overcome the hateful man who had tried to strip her of her dignity. I wondered if Grace had managed the same outcome; I think she had, but she suddenly looked a lot older sitting in the rocking chair, staring into the fire. My eyes drifted to Olivia, who was settled on the floor holding Joy while she slept. She stared at her with rapt attention; maybe she was listening to the talk and maybe not. Anna Beth had told me that her baby sister had been too young to remember much about Mr. Grainger, and we all agreed that was a great blessing.

"Anna Beth, didn't I use t'suck m'fingers jus' like this?" Olivia asked, tearing her eyes away from Joy. She and the baby both had blue eyes and blonde curls in common, too.

"Yes," Anna Beth said softly, smiling at her sister. She had helped raise her, so I knew it meant a tremendous deal to see how much Olivia now loved her daughter.

"We bes' b'gettin' t'bed," Grace sighed, standing from the rocking chair as she wrapped a shawl more tightly around her shoulders. I stood and stretched, furtively watching Anna Beth give Grace an extra-long hug. I turned aside to help Olivia stand with Joy in her arms, giving them their privacy. They had come through terrible times together, a different type of war than mine, and it struck me how we were all survivors in our own ways. *Grace was to Anna Beth as Elliott was to me – without the unsung heroes of our stories, neither of us would have made it out alive. I'd never have met her...* I turned the thoughts over in my mind as we all said goodnight; the possibilities were too painful to consider.

Grace and Olivia left a few days later, and the years continued to fly by. I loved every minute of watching Joy Elizabeth, who at four years old, was growing like a weed. One night, Anna Beth and I were rocking by the fireplace, watching Joy play with a doll on the rug. I smoked a pipe while my wife did a bit of her handiwork, and Joy happily talked to herself, her blonde locks bouncing around her shoulders. I loved those golden curls every bit as much as her Momma's golden-brown waves; their hair shimmered in the sun the same way, like little bits of angel glitter had been sprinkled on them both. Anna Beth had taken much pleasure in making Joy's clothes, but the little mail-order blue dress she wore currently was my absolute favorite. It was the same shade of blue that Anna Beth had worn the night of our infamous picture show date.

With a bittersweet smile, I remembered how I had kissed her for the first time, and she ran out on me! I hated the pain Anna Beth had to experience that night as she told me her hidden truths but also cherished the sincere love that blossomed as a result.

My wife squeezed my hand, bringing me away from Harlan and back to our Edmonson County farmhouse. I rested my pipe on the armrest of the chair and gave her my full attention.

"Mr. Johnston," she whispered quietly, "we're going to have another baby." A smirk crept up the side of her face as I stopped rocking.

"I... how... are you *sure*?" I stuttered. *She has to be kidding! There is no possible way*, I thought to myself, dumbfounded. She couldn't help but laugh, and Joy turned and glanced our way at the sound. Anna Beth smiled at our daughter, who grinned back and continued to play like this was any other ordinary moment.

"I'm as sure as I was when carrying her," my wife replied. "I haven't been as sick with this one, but a babe is definitely stirring within me again."

I ran my hand down my face, the pressure feeling good, then chuckled. "It's *impossible*, Anna Beth. I'm eighty-one years old..." I argued with a shake of my head. She squeezed my hand again, and I hushed.

"*I'm sure*, Mr. Johnston! I went to the doctor yesterday. The Lord is blessing our home again," she assured me. I took one look into those deep, dancing eyes of hers and knew she wouldn't joke about something as marvelous as this!

Michael Anthony was born several months later, and I took special pride in knowing a boy from our miracle marriage would carry on the Johnston name. It was also my hope that he would grow big and strong, so, when I did leave this world, he'd be here to take care of his mother and sister. It was not lost on anyone more than me that my time *must* be short now, *but my stars... why did God continue to bless me so?* I wondered.

On the rare occasion I accompanied my wife and children to church, I'd sit and ask myself that very question again and again. I listened to Brother Ray, the pastor at the time, preach hard about how God sent His son to save all the world's sinners – how He loved us all and only wanted us to believe – but I really wondered how that could be. By their moral standards, I felt I was nothing more than a worm... yet God gave me such good people to share the twilight of my life with! I'd leave the church house partly angry that the service reinforced my feelings of unworthiness and partly yearning to fix myself – to somehow *make* myself worthy of the grace I was experiencing. Everything felt like such a quandary. It didn't take long, however, for me to push the disjointed, nagging feelings down and refocus my energy on my wife and children.

When Michael Anthony was a few months old, Elliott finally came to visit. I laughed to the point of tears when I opened the door and saw him standing on the porch with a box of cigars. He had kept his coming a complete surprise, and I had honestly given up hope I'd ever see him again.

"Well, look what the cat drug in!" I exclaimed, shaking his hand. I pulled him into a tight hug as Anna Beth came in from the kitchen, Michael Anthony in her arms and Joy Elizabeth hiding behind her dress.

"Mr. Foster!" she said. "It's so good to see you!" Anna Beth entertained visitors quite often, but this was the first time someone had come just for me. She looked down at her little shadow with blonde curls and prompted, "Joy, tell Mr. Foster hello. He's one of Papa's oldest friends!"

"Hello," our daughter whispered, twisting a fistful of her momma's dress in her fingers.

"Hello, darling!" Elliott replied with a chuckle, kneeling to look her in the eyes. "You can call me Uncle Elliott!" He held out a gift, and Joy's eyes lit up. She took it cautiously, sat on the floor to unwrap it, and squealed to see a miniature white and purple-flowered tea set.

"Oh, thank you, Uncle Elliott!" Joy exclaimed, getting up to hug his neck. She hurriedly gathered the basket with the little pot and cups and carried them away, no doubt to find her dolls. Elliott stood, holding out a decorative serving dish to Anna Beth with a toy car atop for Michael.

"Well, you still know how to please a crowd," Anna Beth said with a smile. "Thank you for the gifts; you are too kind!"

"You're very welcome, ma'am, and you're right about one thing: this *here* party has turned into a crowd!" Elliott replied with a wink. He pulled the corner of the baby blanket back to better see Michael snuggled in her arms. "You all have a beautiful family... not one, but *two* adorable kids!" My friend looked back at me with a mischievous grin. "You still a young buck, eh?" I laughed, remembering our conversation by the lake the night before I was to be married.

"Would you like to hold him?" Anna Beth asked.

"Oh, I don't think..." Elliott began, raising his hands defensively as he took a step back. Anna Beth gently placed Michael into his arms anyway and patted him on the shoulder. He held the baby awkwardly, his shoulders pressed up against his ears, and it was my turn to chuckle.

"If Mr. Johnston can hold him, you can, too," Anna Beth said simply, turning back toward the kitchen. "Besides, it'll allow me time to get us a piece cake and coffee for an afternoon treat!" she called over her shoulder.

I watched Elliott cradle my son, his shoulders slowly relaxing downward as he stared at Michael's big, blinking eyes – they were both quite curious about the other. Elliott walked toward me, shaking his head.

"My goodness, Daniel, I know you were over the moon about Joy – but a *son*? You really are something!" he proclaimed. "I had to come see it for myself before I croaked… to make sure you weren't telling me tall tales and all."

I knew Elliott didn't have any children; he never even married. He was one of the soldiers that got out of the service and just worked his life away at a mediocre job. I thought of how I had been an aimless wanderer before meeting Anna Beth in the post office of some hole-in-the-wall Kentucky town. She had set my life on a completely different course. It was late in the game of life for me, but this last inning was shaping up to be the best! *Do we all have extended opportunities to turn our lives into something meaningful and some people miss theirs by a narrow margin?* I wondered, hoping my friend had found enough joy in his life to prove it all worthwhile.

"I'm glad you came," I said sincerely, inviting him to take a chair by the fireplace. I lit us each a cigar, and he took a long draw from his.

"Me, too, old chum," he replied, returning his attention to the babe in his arms. "Me, too."

For two weeks, Elliott and I were as inseparable as Anna Beth, Grace, and Olivia when they had been in town. We insisted he take the spare bedroom downstairs instead of renting a hotel room in town, and he and I enjoyed our time together immensely! We took Joy for walks along the stream's edge, watching her squeal and jump from bank to bank where the stream narrowed, and we took turns holding Michael while Anna Beth treated us like kings. She went out of her way to make the most delicious meals, spoiling us with desserts every night. I think our favorite time of day, however, was when Anna Beth was putting the children to bed; we would sit on the porch smoking our pipes and listening to the crickets' song. Ironically, sitting there beside him in the quiet dark reminded me of war, but only the good parts – like when we left the muddy trenches and safely returned to the bivouac, knowing we had given the mission our all.

"You know, I'm going to be seventy-eight years old this month," Elliott confided during one of our last nights together. "I look around here and see all you've built in just a few short years, and it makes a man think. It really does. Where'd my life go? Did I not take enough chances? Did I waste it?" My friend, who usually was so jovial, just stared into the yard while smoking another cigar. Realizing this was not a moment to joke, I cleared my throat uncomfortably.

"I know how you feel, buddy. I was there – that same spot – right before I stopped in Harlan," I replied. "I had been wandering from one place to another without any ambitions... just *existing*. You know how it is. When I think back on that time, I wonder where I would be today if I hadn't seized my chance with Anna Beth. Would my life have meant anything to anybody when I came down to the end of it?"

Elliott dropped his head, rubbing his temples with one hand. "Fighting in the war was probably the only important thing I did with my life, and eventually my little piece in that will be forgotten," he muttered. He sat back in the rocking chair and sighed deeply. "I worked my life away making ends meet, having a bit of good-spirited fun here and there to relieve the pressure... that's about it. Besides our friendship, I don't think anyone will even care when I'm gone."

I looked at my friend, recalling the very real fear of a funeral where no one would come. I had never seen Elliott so depressed, and it worried me in a way I never thought I'd have to worry about him. He was the light-hearted one, a good man, the one who kept *me* on track. "Elliott, you'll be remembered," I said, leaning forward in my rocking chair to see his face better. "What's got you in such a somber mood anyway? You don't usually think about such things."

He shrugged his shoulders and hem hawed around. "Aw, you know... I'm seventy-seven! *You're* eighty-two!" He forced a laugh. "According to nature, our bodies aren't going to make it much longer, old man. I guess coming face to face with that fact makes a man rethink his whole life and the meaning of it all." He shook his head, like the motion could shake away the feeling that threatens to drown us all at one time or another.

I puffed on my pipe and slowly blew the smoke out, letting the stillness of the evening settle around us before speaking again. "I think the whole point of life is to find joy and love," I offered, "in people, in what you do, in life in general. If you can connect with something that gives you that – you've achieved the goal." Elliott glanced at me with pursed lips.

"That sounds like something an *old married man and father of two* would say!" he teased, and I laughed for his sake. I had been dead serious, though.

"Are you feeling okay these days?" I asked. "Any health concerns you're not telling me about?"

"Ah, I'm fine... as good as we *can* feel, you know? Normal aches and pains. How about you?" he countered with a grin. "Are you keeping up with that young wisp of a wife?"

"I feel like a young man in an old man's body," I admitted honestly. "I can't do everything that I used to, and some things I can do aren't up to my satisfaction anymore... but we make it work. Even around the house, I do what my body allows me to do. When strength gives out, I usually pay someone else in town to do whatever! There are a few men from Anna Beth's church that are especially kind to help chop wood and things just to be neighborly. I let them, even though it about kills me to take any kind of charity."

Elliott chuckled. "Yeah, I was kidding you about being a young buck. Young bucks we are not, even if our minds are still as young as they ever were," he agreed. "I don't think I could prance around like a young buck even if it would attract me a lady at this point in the game!" Raucous laughter escaped both of us like a pressure valve release, and we quickly tried to tamp it back down. I knew as accommodating as Anna Beth was, if we woke her and the children, she would skin our hides! After a few more moments of quiet laughter and snide remarks, I stood up. It was getting quite late.

"We best be getting in the house and to our separate corners," I said. "If my doe comes out here after us, you'll be as sorry as me." Elliott obediently followed me to the door, and while we snickered all the way to our beds, I don't believe either of us slept well.

14

I missed Elliott something fierce when he headed back home, fully aware that this visit may very well have been our last. I appreciated James Mutter and all, but he was thirty years my junior. He hadn't seen what I had seen in my lifetime or experienced it for better or worse alongside me. He was born and raised in Edmonson County and had never traveled outside of Kentucky. I had traveled and seen enough in my eighty-two years to appreciate every day as the gift it is. Most men didn't live past their sixties; I had lived another twenty years on borrowed time and was somehow still counting. That's why I spent as much time as I could with Anna Beth and the children.

As Joy Elizabeth and Michael Anthony got older, they turned into exasperating play mates. It was quite amusing, even though Anna Beth wanted me to correct them rather than egg them on. Joy was seven years old to Michael's three, and she would beg him all day long to play dolls, tea party, or house. Of course, the boy would refuse! He was more of a toy truck and rocks kind of fella, which Joy had zero interest in. However, he *always* fell asleep first, and Joy loved to sneak out of her room and put her doll's bonnet on his head, tying it as tight as she dared under his pudgy chin without waking him. I had never heard such wailing and gnashing of teeth as when Michael would wake up with that blasted bonnet on! Anna Beth would fuss at Joy Elizabeth and tell her to apologize, then she'd fuss at Michael Anthony and tell him if he would just play *one* of his sister's games occasionally, she wouldn't go to such measures, and I would just sit back and laugh until she cut those Momma eyes toward me. Then it was the *kids'* turn to laugh, and everyone would be happy again... except Momma!

One time, Anna Beth got so fit-to-be-tied at us kids – me included – she threw her hands up in the air, stormed off the porch, and spent the rest of the morning at Rose's house. The kids were a little bewildered by her absence at first, but I gave them leftover cake for breakfast and took them to play by the stream, and all was well. I sat on a rock and watched them laugh and splash each other, scaring away any fish that dared come near. They were captivating to watch, those children of mine, their life and energy waxing as mine waned. I could live vicariously through them all day! When their mother rounded the bend on her way home and saw us all there, her still irritated countenance softened considerably. She ended up pulling off her boots and wading into the stream with the kids, and they were *all* soaked by the end of the water fight that ensued. The image of their huge, wet smiles was one of my fondest memories.

One summer evening, I was reminiscing back on that day at the stream when Anna Beth found me on the porch. She quietly shut the door behind her, and I had a flashback of Clara bringing me a glass of tea while saying I could rest as long as I needed to. I shook it from my mind, shifting in my chair uncomfortably; resentment often bubbled up alongside regret.

"The kids are finally asleep," Anna Beth whispered, coming to sit on the arm of my rocker.

I wrapped my arm around her waist and breathed in her sweet scent as she relaxed against me. Even now, almost ten years married, there was still a comfortable beauty about her that heightened my senses. It was a *know-you-to-the-core-and-love-you-anyway* kind of thing. She loved me despite my flaws, and perhaps that is why I was still so smitten.

"Thank you for your help today. Just playing checkers with Michael and listening to Joy go on and on about her play schemes allowed me time to get some things done. I don't know what I would do without you," she said, wrapping her arm around my shoulders. I patted her leg. At some point, she would *have* to live without me... but I didn't have to remind her of that right now. "What are you thinking about?" she asked after a moment of silence.

I pushed my worries for the future away and grinned as I rehashed the story of the stream shenanigan. "I can still see your face as you rounded the bend! You were upset with all three of us, but you looked around and consciously chose joy," I recalled. "It's one of the many things I love about you. You always choose to look on the bright side of things."

She laughed and playfully slapped my knee. "Well, if you had helped me *parent* that morning instead of egging those two on, I wouldn't have lost my cool and gone to Rose's to blow off steam! I don't consider that looking for the bright side all the time..."

I pulled Anna Beth into my lap, wrapping both arms around her waist as we laughed together. Looking into her eyes, I saw myself – that vulnerable, sullen, broken man turned into a tender husband and father, and a sudden gush of love welled up within me. Her hair was messy and slipping out of her braid; she was no doubt tired from mothering all day, but I leaned in and kissed her anyway. I could feel her surprise give way to comfort. She wrapped her arms around my neck and kissed back. It was gentle and warm, and my body started to tingle like an old electrical wire that still had a spark. It had been quite a while since I had last felt desire; the gaps between our intimacy naturally growing farther apart as my body wore out over the years. Anna Beth never complained about such things; she was such a good wife in that way. She always seemed satisfied with whatever I could give and didn't value one act of love over another.

Anna Beth pulled away first and rested her head on my shoulder. "You changed my whole life, Mr. Johnston. Do you really *know* that?" she asked quietly. "Before you, I was doing my best to live life despite my demons – trying to quiet my own pain by helping other children through theirs. I realized, though, when that little girl was lost in the woods and no one could find her, I was in way over my head." She paused as I recalled the story of her final teaching days in North Carolina. One of her students, abused by her drunken father, escaped a house fire and the whole town had to search for her. Luckily, a Native American girl who Anna Beth had befriended knew the woods well, and they found the missing student alive.

"It's difficult to explain that part of my life," she continued, "but it's like I had let go of God's hand and wandered around on my own a bit – like wandering around in the woods looking for Jenny – so when we found her, I understood how much I needed to get back to what I knew was right. That's why I went back to Harlan... the place that first broke me and where God fixed me up again. I just needed to start over with some things."

I cleared my throat, unsure why she felt the need to tell me all this right now. "I'm glad you went back to Harlan – if you hadn't, I never would have found you."

"I know I still struggle sometimes with my past, but I don't think anyone else could have helped me the way you have. I haven't had nightmares about Mr. Grainger in years now; I guess because I finally feel safe," Anna Beth added. "You've given me such a wonderful life, and those babies..." she paused to smile, "it's like our love spilled over and made them so we could enjoy life together even *more*! The whole thing has just been a miracle of God." She looked up at me, and I kissed her again with all the tenderness I had.

When our lips pulled a part, I decided it was my turn to confide my feelings. "I've thought the same thing many times over... except it's *you* who changed *my* whole life," I pointed out, gently rocking us back and forth. After a few moments, she sat up and smirked at me. Ten years together, and she still had that cute, irresistible grin.

"Let's head to bed," she proposed, standing up and reaching for my hand. I knew what she meant, and it made me chuckle.

"Angel, I don't think...," I started to say.

"It's okay, Mr. Johnston," she interrupted, her voice lilting upwards into a tease. "I will *never* force you to do anything you do not want to do. You can set the pace between us. I'm older now, and I've had many happy years. Love comes in all forms; I'll follow anywhere you lead."

I stared at my witty wife, taking in the whole wonderful sight of her, as she turned my words on me from our wedding night so long ago. I had known the sentiments I spoke with sincerity had meant the world to her then, and her continued devotion meant the world to me now. She was as persuasive as she was gorgeous, so of course, I retired with her, arm in arm – come what may.

We were both glad we seized the moment, too, because about a month later, I fell ill like never before. I had always been relatively healthy; the only illness I remembered laying me flat was chicken pox in my early youth. My body was more achy than usual, though, and it seemed like I couldn't catch my breath. Anna Beth noticed my wheezing right away and told me to stay in the first-floor bedroom to rest. She telephoned Rose, and James came with the doctor. He examined me, pulled the covers back up to my chest, and turned to take Anna Beth out of the room. I called him back with a wave of my hand and rattled cough, however, slightly perturbed at his tactlessness.

"I'm not in the grave yet, Doc," I wheezed, concentrating hard on slowly breathing in and out. "Whatever you're going to tell my wife, you tell me."

The doctor stuck his hands deep in his pockets with hesitation but then addressed us both. "It seems you've come down with the nastiest kind of cold, Mr. Johnston – it's moved into your lungs. They call it bronchitis. It will be difficult to rid you of it." Anna Beth stiffened with the news.

"How do we treat it?" she asked. I watched her cross her arms in determination and knew she intended to fight for my life.

"Well, it's not easy, and even then, there are no promises at his age," the doctor sighed.

"I'll worry about hope and faith, Doctor; you tell me what to physically do," my wife insisted.

"Bed rest in a well-ventilated room such as this will definitely help," he said, motioning around the downstairs bedroom. "A light diet and steam inhalations are also beneficial in turning the tide. If the fever subsides, he will need sunshine, fresh air, nourishing food... and he needs to exercise his breathing morning and night. The road to full recovery is a long one, but just keeping it from turning into pneumonia is enough to worry about for now."

I slept a lot in the months following, but Anna Beth was at my side every time I woke. She fed me a spoonful of broth at a time when I could eat, and thrice a day she covered my head with a towel so I could breathe deeply over a steaming pan of hot water. This, she hoped and prayed, would open my lungs and avoid pneumonia. My wife worked tirelessly and started to look pretty worn around the edges. When I was cognizant enough, I hated that I couldn't get out of bed and help her with the housework or kids – who seemed to be unnaturally quiet. I inquired once as to their whereabouts, and learned Rose was keeping them during the days. Anna Beth said not to worry about anything other than building my strength back up, and we both returned to the individual work that now consumed our days.

The wicked cough racked my whole frame, making every inch of me ache. My fever came and went as my body valiantly fought the infection. At the lowest point, I finally succumbed to the fact that my end was close. It had to be. The thought I hated more than leaving the love of my life and our children, however, was how Anna Beth was having to care for me these last days. I was supposed to be caring for her... but we both knew this turn of events was always inevitable. It was the price to pay for loving each other fifty years apart.

One afternoon, I stirred awake to find Anna Beth sitting in a chair at my bedside. She had laid her head on her arms atop the quilt near my right hand and was fast asleep. She felt me shift, and her eyes fluttered open.

"How are you feeling?" she asked, sitting up to take my hand in hers. She kissed my knuckles and let her cheek rest against my open palm.

"About the same," I muttered, squeezing the words out before descending into a coughing fit. When I caught my breath, her concerned eyes were boring a hole in me.

"Mr. Johnston, you're not giving up on me, are you? On us? The kids? Your life?" my wife asked frankly. She bit her quivering lip, afraid of the answer. I furrowed my brow, hoping to say something that would be of comfort to my soon-to-be widowed wife.

"Of course not, Angel... I want to stay here with you as long as I can, but I think we both know I've long overstayed my welcome on this earth," I managed to rasp out.

"That's *nonsense!*" She spit the words at me, suddenly more angry than afraid. I was taken aback by her sudden burst of emotion, not able to recall her ever having a cross word toward me. "Not a single one of us know when our time is going to be, or how much life we still have left to live – only God knows such things!"

I opened my mouth to speak again, but Anna Beth took my hand and held it firmly against her stomach. I could feel a slight bump under her blouse, a swelling I hadn't noticed all the long weeks before.

"You may *think* your time is over," she continued, tears streaming down her cheeks, "but *this* little one's time is just beginning on earth. Don't you want to meet our last child?"

Tears welled up in my own eyes, and my feeble breath caught in my throat. We had used up all our luck and then some just to get Joy and Michael. *A third child?* I thought feverishly. *But we hadn't....* The possibility of her being unfaithful, however, was not an option. "Anna Beth... when?" I whispered questionably.

"You *know* when," my wife insisted, still holding my hand to her stomach. "That night I sat in your lap on the front porch, and you kissed me so gently – the night we told each other how much we changed one another's lives... that all of this...," she motioned around the room to encompass our whole lives, "is a miracle most people could never believe."

I gently rubbed my thumb across Anna Beth's stomach, sobbing in my own disbelief. My tears wet the pillow under my weak head. That little life inside her was half mine, and if I didn't recover from this illness, I would only be a story to him or her.

"*Live*, Mr. Johnston," Anna Beth pleaded. "Live to see *this* child." She crawled into bed next to me and laid her head in the crook of my shoulder, both of us crying together. All I could do was hold her; I was too weak to say another word.

The probability of me coming out of this alive was slim, but I *wanted* to see that child and for that child to see me. I closed my eyes and figured it didn't hurt to whisper a prayer to the God who created this world and all that was in it, to the God I knew Anna Beth served with all her heart, soul, mind, and strength, the God I wished I knew better. I mouthed the words silently while my wife cried into my chest: *Dear Lord, pease let me live. Let me see this last bit of joy You've sent our way. I know I'm not worthy of any favors, but if You see the sparrow fall and love me as much as Brother Ray says You do, maybe You will be merciful. Could You give me just a little more time? If You do, maybe I can search for You the way Anna Beth says she did... she says she knows for sure You are real because she feels Your holy spirit. If that's a possibility, if there truly is a way to make it to shore – be my lighthouse and show me the way.*

15

While the illness took its toll, I must have found grace in God's sight because I did slowly but surely regain strength. I knew only the hand of the Almighty could bring me back from the brink of death at eighty-five years old to see our third and final child, Louisa Rose, come into this world. As many happy days as I had shared with Anna Beth, Joy, and Michael, this babe's birth was extra special. I had *lived* to see this child!

Everyone else loved Louisa from the moment they saw her, too. Her hair was more cinnamon brown with gold highlights like her momma's, yet it was curly like Joy's. The mixture of the two made the glittering effect bounce off in all directions, like little shining ringlets vibrating with energy. Joy Elizabeth was ecstatic to have a real baby sister to dress up and play house with, too, and Michael was relieved to finally be left alone to play in the dirt and climb trees. Anna Beth was also naturally smitten; she knew this child would be the last spillover of our immense love for each other. If anyone was happier than me, though, it was Rose Mutter, Louisa's namesake. If Rose hadn't taken our children in so Anna Beth could nurse me back to health, I probably wouldn't have survived to see another day. Rose bought Louisa a tiny white smocked dress with little red roses all over the hem from the *Lee's Catalogue*, a significant purchase for her and James, and was very proud when Anna Beth dressed the babe in it for church on her first trip to town.

We telephoned Anna Beth's family to tell them of all our good fortune, both my renewed health and the birth of our second daughter, but like always, I chose to write Elliott a letter. I wished he could come for another visit; I longed to sit on the porch and talk the night away with him again. Last I heard, however, he had fallen and was in the Highland County Hospital in Virginia. He had told me not to worry, that it was just a couple of broken bones – and he had seen worse in war – but I *did* worry. I hoped my letter found him back on his feet, and like me, he had a bit more time left on this old earth.

Louisa Rose was toddling along in no time at all; she could amble about as fast as I could with my cane. The bronchitis had taken its toll on my already aged and battered body, and my muscles were weakened considerably. I didn't complain, however. I was just as thankful to get out of bed in the mornings as curious little Louisa bouncing in her crib... except I didn't bounce anymore.

For this and various other reasons, I took to saying Louisa and I were cut from the same cloth. We both wanted to do more than we were able but still had fun doing whatever we could manage! For instance, if Louisa didn't get her way, she'd wail on the floor until Anna Beth or Joy came to pick her up; occasionally, Michael would even take pity and toss her a toy to stop the tears. I, on the other hand, was a sophisticated fusser... I would just kindly call the others until they came to see what I needed. Anna Beth took to leaving Louisa in my vicinity and jokingly told each of us to watch the other. Louisa and I would make eye contact and grin. She would crawl over to me, pull herself up on my cane, and off we'd go, both of us holding onto it for support as we made slow, intentional steps forward. That's how she learned to walk!

Anna Beth would also drop her into my arms while I was rocking on the porch in the evenings, so she could have a few quiet moments to tuck in Joy and Michael without a baby underfoot. Louisa and I would sit there completely content, rocking, singing, and pointing out animals and such until her eyelids fell with the dusk. Anna Beth would come back out with a sincere smile of relief, brush the untamed curls from Louisa's face, and kiss me in appreciation. I'd watch her roll the baby back into her arms, and I always smiled to myself as she carried her back inside to the bedroom. I knew she could have easily put all three children to bed without my help, but she always found ways to make me feel needed, no matter how feeble I grew.

One late spring day, when the trees had all budded out and were steadying themselves for summer, Anna Beth found me by the barn.

My Tin Lizzie had stopped running a few years back, and even though we had upgraded to a Mercury Club Coup for the whole family, I still liked to tinker with the Model-T in my free time. I guess I was trying to bring the old hunk of metal back to life like God did me.

Things weren't going in my favor, however, when she entered the barn. I was trying to put part of the engine back together with a screwdriver but couldn't hold my hands steady enough to keep pressure on the tool and twist! I didn't feel frustrated with myself very often, but when the helpless feeling did bubble up, it felt like I was drinking acid. Not being able to *do* things I wanted to do burned me through and through. *My mind is clear as a bell; it's just this old body that's letting me down!* I fumed. It wasn't even that I minded asking for help or even paying people to come in and do things from time to time; it was just sometimes a man wanted to take care of things himself... no matter how old he got.

"What are you doing?" Anna Beth asked quietly, clasping her hands behind her as she leaned against the barn's door frame. She didn't glance at the fumbling screwdriver and engine part in my hand, bless her; she just kept her eyes on my face with that gentle, unconditional acceptance I so appreciated.

"Aw, nothing much – just trying to fix this part for the old Tin Lizzie. My hands aren't cooperating, though," I told her, trying to assuage my anger and keep my voice steady. If she had been Clara, she would have told me to rest and let someone else do that work... or worse yet, she would have taken the screwdriver from my hands and done it herself, thinking that was the kindest service.

Anna Beth nodded. "I'm sure you'll get it," she replied with a confidence that felt like a balm to my nerves. Whether she believed it to be the truth, I cared not – it was love in disguise. "Would you fancy taking a break and walking into town with me and the kids?"

I knew such an offer was more love in disguise. It would take Anna Beth *triple* the time to go to town and back if the kids and I were in tow, yet she was standing here ready to make the journey with a smile on her face. She was simply a jewel, so how could I say no?

"I'd like that," I said with a smile, wiping my greasy hands on an old towel. I threw it down on the counter and retrieved my cane from the wall, starting toward my wife. I paused by her at the door and murmured into her ear, "Thank you, Angel."

"You're most welcome, Mr. Johnston," she whispered respectfully, looping her arm in mine. I patted her hand gently. It was something to think the woman nicknamed Dignity so long ago was helping preserve *my* dignity all these years later.

We gathered the children who had been playing on the tire swing in the yard and made our way toward the stream. Anna Beth let me set the pace with my cane and encouraged the children to explore the holler as we leisurely strolled. "Let's not get in the water on the way to town, kids," she reminded them firmly. "You don't want to be wet as we go in and out of the stores. If you all are well behaved, you can walk in the stream on the way home."

The kids nodded their acknowledgement and ran on in front of us. Joy Elizabeth, who was ten years old and now stood past my elbow, took Louisa Rose by the hand as they scurried off to the right. Louisa had just turned two and had happily advanced to trying to keep up with her sister and brother. I missed the days she held onto my cane, but I was proud of her tenacity all the same. Michael Anthony, who was a strong six-year-old with a natural sense of the outdoors, jutted off to the left toward the stream. He jumped it at a narrow part and walked along the opposite bank in his own solitude. I watched him survey the ground until he found the perfect walking stick, then he held it up for us to admire.

"Look, Papa! I have a walking stick like you!" he called with a big grin.

"That's a mighty fine one, son!" I called back.

I spotted a purple flower poking out of the moist spring ground, sandwiched between a rock and log, and with effort, I leaned down to pluck it up for Anna Beth. She accepted it with a knowing grin and slipped it behind her ear, then took my hand and held it all the way to town.

When we arrived, Anna Beth took the girls and disappeared inside the mercantile. She needed fabric for some dresses she wanted to make, so Michael and I sat outside on the bench, people-watching. Men would wave or tip their hats with the occasional hello. Women would nod and smile kindly. All their eyes would linger on us a little longer than normal, reminding me of the first years Anna Beth and I were together. Everyone in town now knew of the Johnstons: the man who married a girl fifty years his junior and together had three children. They all knew Michael was my son... but I, too, admit his six years to my eighty-eight was a bit of a sight.

Our family's vast age differences never bothered our children as far as I could tell. Kids don't care how old you are. As long as you love them, they love you right back – no judgments or conditions. I patted Michael's leg, and he leaned his head over on my arm, probably tired of waiting for the ladies. He twirled a leaf by the stem between his fingers like I had so often seen Anna Beth do with little branches on our walks. He had a lot of her in him – the quiet, gritty, heroic part, and some of me, too – the loner part.

He sat up suddenly, startling me from my thoughts. "Hey, Papa, can I go check the post office? Maybe Uncle Elliott wrote us a letter!" he exclaimed.

"Go ahead," I nodded with a chuckle. He darted off the porch, jumped the steps in one swoop, and landed with a greenstick agility I envied. I was watching him run down the street to the post office when James came walking up the sidewalk.

"Howdy, Daniel!" he said, shaking my hand. "I saw y'little fella there; he's headed somewheres fas'! What brings y'all t'town? You're lookin' good, ole friend!" I had only come to town a few times since my bout with bronchitis, and even then, I hadn't stayed out long.

"Hey, James," I said with a smile, scooting over so he could sit next to me for a spell. "Anna Beth needed some fabric, and I fancied the walk. We've been missing you and Rose, you all should come over sometime for supper," I offered. We had gotten out of our habit of alternating weekend suppers, and I knew Anna Beth especially would love to spend time with our friends again.

"That would b'wonderful, n'then if y'feel up t'it, y'all can come b'our house next time," James replied. "Maybe Anna Beth could bring that delicious apple pie she's known fo'." He winked at me, and I laughed. James loved the pie Anna Beth made from Grace's special recipe; she had really made a name for herself here in Edmonson County between her good home cooking *and* being married to me.

"Papa! Papa!" Michael busted out of the post office and excitedly ran across the street. He was waving a letter in his hand, and my heart jumped to think it was from Elliott. I hadn't heard from him at all in the last year! Inwardly, I had worried he had passed, and no one would have known to tell me… it wasn't like he had a next of kin I could contact to check up on him. I had pushed the thought far from my mind, however, and still wrote him monthly, hoping to hear a response – any response – soon.

Michael bounded up the steps and handed me the envelope while James looked over my shoulder curiously. My son put his hands on his hips, proud of his fruitful trip, and breathed heavily. "It's not from Uncle Elliott, Papa. It's got Momma's name on it and Aunt Martha's return address... but look, that's not Martha's name." He pointed to the name carefully penned in the top left corner of the envelope.

My breath caught in my throat as I leaned forward, studying the envelope in disbelief. "Michael Anthony, go fetch your momma, please," I mumbled quietly.

Michael took one look at my stunned face and said, "Yes, sir – right away, Papa!" and off he ran on another important mission.

James's curiosity immediately turned to concern. "Is ev'rythin' all right?" he asked. I handed him the envelope, and he shrugged his shoulders. "Who's *Laura Atwood*?"

I looked at my friend for a long moment, considering what to say. I decided the truth was best in a situation like this; Anna Beth had always been honest about the past, even her private matters, when she had a heart to tell people.

"That there is a letter from Anna Beth's long-lost mother," I said quietly. The words sounded as foreign coming out of my mouth as the name looked on the envelope.

"But we met 'er mother, Grace," James said, confused, "n'er sister, Olivia."

"Olivia is her sister, but Grace is their foster mother. Her real parents parceled her and her sisters – there were two others – out among strangers when they moved to Harlan County. They left a fifth sister in Missouri. They were completely broke and promised they'd come back for the kids when they got on their feet... then they just *disappeared*," I explained as best I could. "Anna Beth got one letter early on from her mother but never heard from them again. Grace raised her and Olivia as her own."

James shook his head in shock, understanding my sudden apprehension. "You're serious? I had no idea! T'live all that time n'not know what happened t'y'fam'ly... how long has it been?"

I sighed deeply. "Twenty-three years," I said. I thought about how many years it had been since I had left my children; *what would they think if I did send a letter after all this time?* I pondered.

Anna Beth barely mentioned her parents anymore, but I knew she still thought about them because every August she would have a severe quiet spell. She'd get out of bed and go through the motions of our life, but her heart would be far from us. I was patient and just picked up the slack, because I knew her parents had dropped her off at the Graingers' farm in August, promising to come back by Christmas. It was an anniversary of sorts for her; she was still counting the years, too.

16

Anna Beth held the envelope with trembling hands as we walked out of town. She carefully opened it when we got to the stream's edge and read the letter inside multiple times, completely lost in her own thoughts. I watched with concern as she seemingly regressed to that twelve-year-old who didn't know which way was home. If it were me, I didn't know what I would make of it, either... *twenty-three years* without word from your parents, and then one day the letter you've always hoped for comes.

I gave the kids permission to pull their shoes off and play in the stream, and they happily stuffed their stockings inside their boots, tied their laces to drape the shoes around their necks, and ran off. Walking close to my wife for support but also trying to give her some space, I occasionally called to Joy and Michael to hold Louisa's hand. Our littlest one had already fallen face first in the water; Anna Beth hadn't even noticed. We walked all the way home in that uncomfortable silence, me listening to the kids' laughter drifting back to us from somewhere upstream, and her immersed in another time and place altogether. I didn't ask her to share what was in the letter, either. I could tell she was disappointed by her disapproving scowl – a person needs more of an explanation than what can fit into a few, condensed lines of black ink – but I knew when she was ready to discuss its contents, she would seek me out.

When our farmhouse came into view, Anna Beth folded the letter and slipped it into her pocket. She busied herself with the evening routine of fixing supper, giving the children their baths, and finally tucking them into bed – all with the fewest necessary words and forced smiles, but with extra tender kisses. I sat on the porch smoking my pipe, waiting. I knew my wife. She wouldn't sit alone with this much longer, even if just sharing her thoughts meant processing them out loud. When she finally opened the screen door at dusk, I nodded my acknowledgement. As she closed the door quietly and leaned against it, I saw the anguish, anger, and long-overdue relief etched in her features; I knew it was a battle between the positive and negative warring within her – I had been there many times. I watched her with deep concern mixed with a hint of curiosity. *What does a parent have to say to their child after twenty-three years?* I wondered.

"Twenty-three years, Mr. Johnston," Anna Beth sighed. She reached up and roughly tugged her hair out of its braid, running her fingers through the loosened waves. I patted the porch swing next to me, and she came and sank onto it. Instinctively, I rested my hand on her leg, hoping it provided a bit of comfort and stability to a carefully constructed world collapsing in her mind.

"I know what happened," she continued, tears finally gathering in her eyes. She buried her face in her hands and, with a muffled voice, spoke through her fingers. "My parents had to go several counties away to find work like we all figured, and *Daddy*," she said, choking on the memory of him before catching her breath to go on, "my daddy died in one of the mine explosions. If my mother has the year right, I was about thirteen when it happened." She let her hands slip into her lap and shrugged, her face wet with tears. I wrapped my arm around her shoulders, not knowing what to say.

"Momma came back to Harlan to gather us girls, but she didn't have a penny to her name," she persisted. "She was sleeping in the woods and begging for scraps, hoping to find some kind of seamstress work so she could support us. Do you know that she *came* to the Graingers' farm to *tell* me what happened?" she asked incredulously. "She saw me in the fields working and Olivia happily playing on the front porch and just decided it was better to leave us all in foster care where at least we got meals and a bed! She said it would have been a rough and miserable life if she took us with her on the road...." Anna Beth pulled out of my grasp and looked at me with the wild eyes of a cornered animal; we both knew how rough and miserable her life had been *because* her parents didn't come back. "Can you *believe* that?" she whispered disdainfully. I reached to gather her into me again and she only resisted a moment before crumpling into my chest with an excruciating sob.

"She was that *close* and didn't tell me!" she cried. "She could have *told* me about Daddy and explained how she thought staying with the Graingers would be best... but no, she just left me to wonder all these years and think the worst! She let me think I was unwanted! She didn't even pick my letters up from the mercantile because she thought it better for us to never know she had even come back... how could a mother *do* that?" Anna Beth fell quiet for a moment, drawing in a deep breath. "I think about Joy, Michael, and Louisa; I could *never....*"

I held her tightly, letting her weep. It killed me to see someone who had worked all her life to pull herself together break into pieces again. If I could take the pain from her, absorb it into myself and compartmentalize it next to the war, I would.

"If she had taken me with her when I was thirteen," she spoke into my chest, "I wouldn't have been *raped*. I would have been gone from that wretched place before he ever laid a hand on me!"

I kissed the top of her head and started to swing us gently back and forth, still at a complete loss for words. I didn't want to admit it to Anna Beth, but I identified – at least in part – with her mother. I thought leaving my family was best for everyone involved, also... but what if something terrible had befallen my children because of my choices? *Can you forgive yourself for what you don't know even happened? Can they forgive you for leaving when they never will fully understand why?* My own questions swirled inside my head, mixing with my wife's grief.

Eventually, Anna Beth sat up and took another deep, steadying breath. She swiped her tears with the back of her hand, and I knew she was collecting herself at last. "Just this last year my mother finally went back to Harlan and picked up the bundle of letters I had left for her and Daddy," she confided. "Momma said she got to a better place in her life and *had* to know what became of her girls... *her* girls... doesn't she understand we stopped being hers the moment she abandoned us?" Anna Beth chuckled at the bitter resolution of everything she had speculated about for so long. I knew other kids had teased her, taunting that she was an orphan – and knowing they had been right had to be like salt in her wound.

"The last letter I wrote her, when we were leaving for Tennessee after Mr. Grainger's trial, she kept quoting from it. She said since I would always wonder what happened and why they didn't come back, she decided she needed to find us girls and tell us the truth once and for all. I had told her in my letter that I forgave her of *everything*, and she said that's what gave her the courage to finally track us down again. Martha was easy to find, and from her she found the rest of us. She left Martha and Janie after a visit a month ago, was planning to see Emily next, then come here to see me, and on to Tennessee to visit Olivia."

"She's coming *here*?" I asked, surprised. A letter was one thing, but a visit was something else altogether. "Are you okay with that?"

Anna Beth leaned forward with one arm wrapped tightly around her stomach and the other hand cradling her bowed head. "I don't *know*. I just… I don't know if I even *want* to see her now. Does that make me a terrible person?" she asked quietly, briefly glancing at me with red, swollen eyes. After all the emotions she had experienced that day, guilt seemed the most unfair. I gently rubbed her back as she buried her face in her hands again.

"*You* are an amazing, generous, and loving person *despite* how you grew up," I replied sincerely. "This woman left you in someone else's care and horrible things happened because of it. I know you've made peace with your past as much as you could, but now that you know the rest of the story… I can understand how it opens old wounds that have long been seared over." Anna Beth sat up, looking toward the stream. We could only see lightening bugs dancing in the darkness, but, if you listened, you could hear the little rush of water not far off.

"That's exactly how I feel. I may have forgiven her *then*, but now there's more to forgive," she said solemnly. Our eyes connected, and I watched hers fill with a hardness I had never seen there before. "I don't know that I'm strong enough to forgive her a second time."

I pulled my wife back into an embrace and held her for a long time. She finally seemed drained of emotion, but I held onto her anyway, just listening to her breathe. When the moon rose high overhead, she suggested we try to sleep. I obediently walked her into the house, my cane in one hand with her tucked under my free arm, and we made our way to the first-floor bedroom. We had stayed in that room during my bronchitis spell, and even though she said it was because we needed the ones upstairs for Joy and Michael to have their own space, I knew it was so I wouldn't have to do the steps anymore. It was another bit of love in disguise, yet I was at a loss for how to reciprocate all her kindnesses in this moment.

Anna Beth changed into her gown and climbed under the covers, and I pulled the quilt up to her chin before changing myself. I was careful not to wake Louisa, who still slept in a crib in the corner of our room. Once settled and as the tension in my back released, I opened my arm so my wife could nestle into my chest again. It was a comfortable routine for the two of us, except this night, and several more to come, she cried herself to sleep while I lay awake with worry.

A week later, while Anna Beth and the children were visiting Rose for one of her grandchildren's birthday parties, Mrs. Laura Atwood did indeed show up on our doorstep. I opened the door to a tall, thin woman in her late fifties and took a step back. She was dressed nicely, but the deep grooves in her leathery face exposed a lifetime of pain and regret. I knew her immediately; she, Anna Beth, and the other sisters strongly favored each other.

"Good afte'noon," she spoke quietly, clutching her purse. She looked quite anxious, like she didn't know how to proceed. As she cleared her throat, she stood a little taller. "I'm looking for Anna Beth Atwood Johnston."

"Well, you have the right house," I said flatly, stepping onto the porch while pulling the screen door shut behind me. Anna Beth had yet to tell me if she even wanted to see her mother, so I knew better than to invite her into our home.

"Are y'Mr. Johnston?" she asked, her eyes assessing me up and down. They lingered on my cane, and I squeezed the handle of it until my knuckles turned white. *Had any of Anna Beth's sisters told her I was old enough to be Anna Beth's grandfather?* I wondered. Our age difference hadn't felt judged in quite a while, and the defensiveness I felt took me off guard.

"Yes, I'm Daniel Johnston. I married your daughter about thirteen years ago," I answered directly. The woman's eyes widened in surprise, whether that I knew her or by our unconventional marriage, I wasn't sure.

"So, y'was expectin' me... I trust Anna Beth received m'letter, then?" she asked, recovering herself quickly.

"She did," I confirmed. I wanted to tell her how Anna Beth had suffered since then but decided it wasn't my place to get in the middle of whatever was left of their relationship.

"Is she home?" she asked, leaning around me to peer into the house through a window.

"No, she's out," I replied, crossing my arms protectively.

Laura Atwood took a deep breath and looked me straight in the eyes for the first time. There was an earnestness about her stare that reminded me so much of my wife; I could have been staring at an older version of her.

"Mr. Johnston, I know y'mus' think m'husband n'I were awful people t'leave our children with strangers n'not come back for 'em," she said, drawing herself up to full stature with a shadow of confidence. "But we had our reasons, we had a plan, n'then when he passed so suddenly – I... I jus' didn't see any way t'support 'em by m'self. I'm sure even though Anna Beth says she forgave me, she still has hard feelin's t'handle. I'm expectin' that." Her eyes brimmed with tears, but she blinked them back with great self-control. "It was her childhood after all. I... I jus' want t'see m'children 'gain... tell 'em I'm sorry n'that I wish we had it t'do over. I want t'tell 'em once more 'fore I die that they *were* loved. I want 'em t'remember us how we were, not what they imagined, even if the truth hurts."

My heart softened toward this woman; we had both left our children, and I *did* understand wanting to make amends before one dies. I, too, had wanted to ensure my life had mattered somehow and that I wouldn't be forgotten. With a sigh, I motioned to one of the rocking chairs on the porch. "You can have a seat if you like. I'll get you a glass of water. Anna Beth and the children should be home soon," I replied.

As she seated herself, I went inside and called James and Rose. I hoped to warn Anna Beth that her mother had arrived in her absence, but James said she and the kids had already left for home. I sat the receiver in its cradle and stared at the photograph of our wedding day hanging over the sideboard. My wife's face had been shining with such radiant joy; our union was a new beginning for her as much as it was for me. I glanced back toward the porch. I didn't want anything or anyone to threaten who she had become by dredging up a tumultuous history long buried... but I also knew this was out of my hands. The woman was here, and there would be a reckoning. With a shake of my head, I made my way to the kitchen for that glass of water, walking slowly to the rhythmic thumping of my cane.

After handing the glass of water to Mrs. Atwood, I stood at the porch steps, leaning against the post with my back to her. She took a few sips before setting it on the table in between the rockers. I kept my eyes toward the stream, knowing Anna Beth and the kids would be coming up between the thicket of trees and into the clearing any moment.

"So, y've met Anna Beth's sisters? I'm comin' from Emily's house, but I saw Martha n'Janie first. They say they've all met ya, n'that y'n'Anna Beth have three children," the woman tried to engage me in conversation. "When I leave here, I'll go on t'see m'youngest, Olivia, all though I'm sure she don't 'member me... she was only two when we lef' Missouri."

"Yes, I've met her sisters and Grace," I answered simply, keeping my eyes on the tree line, "and Anna Beth and I have three children together."

"Y'are a man o'few words, Mr. Johnston," she observed. "M'husband was also."

"Sometimes we don't have much to say," I said, crossing my arms again.

I heard her pick the water glass back up from the table right as I spotted Louisa's curly head bounding between the trees. She was quickly followed by Michael, who had his arms out like an airplane whizzing through the air. A moment later, Joy and Anna Beth came into view, holding hands and most likely rehashing the party fun. When Anna Beth looked up and saw me, recognition stiffened her posture. Even from a distance, I could see her face pale as she slowed slightly. Joy looked up at her questioningly. I nodded at my wife – one solid _you can do this_ dip – and she continued to put one foot in front of another, turning to say something to Joy Elizabeth. Our oldest daughter let go of her mother's hand and ran ahead to gather Michael and Louisa, holding them back, until they could all walk up the porch steps together. When the kids noticed the stranger in the rocking chair, Joy pulled Louisa onto her hip and took Michael by the hand.

"Well, look at that," Mrs. Atwood whispered, standing up. She swallowed hard, not able to take her eyes off Joy. "She looks so much like ya, Anna Beth, n'carryin' that youngin 'round on her hip like y'did Livie!"

"You know Aunt Livie?" Michael asked curiously.

"I do, young man... I ain't seen her in a _very_ long time, but I want t'really soon," she answered.

Anna Beth, who had positioned herself behind the children, placed one hand on Joy's shoulder and the other on Michael's as she cleared her throat. I suspected she was steeling herself for the first spoken words since she told her mother goodbye all those years ago. "Kids, this is your Grandma Laura," she said, avoiding her mother's eyes and looking at me instead. "This here is Joy Elizabeth, Michael Anthony, and Louisa Rose," she said, introducing the children.

"We have another grandma?" Joy asked, looking up at Anna Beth. "Other than Grandma Grace?" Mrs. Atwood looked taken aback by her questions, no doubt realizing that her daughter had *never* spoken her name around the children.

Anna Beth's mouth pursed into a tight line. We had naturally let the kids assume Grace was Anna Beth's biological mother and their only grandmother on purpose; they did not need to be burdened with such painful family history until they were much older. I now cleared my throat; you could cut the tension on that porch with a knife.

"Come on, children – let's go inside and let Momma get reacquainted with Grandma Laura. They haven't seen each other for a very long time," I suggested. I ushered the children inside, got the younger two settled with some toys, and started a game of checkers with Joy.

Through the open window, I could hear the women's silence finally give way to short sentences and then fast, whispered talk. I heard both crying at some point and turned the radio on so the kids wouldn't hear. As it neared supper time, I enlisted Joy's help with frying chicken, Michael's with mashing potatoes, and little Louisa set the table for six, just in case Anna Beth invited her mother in.

When we just about had the meal on the table, Anna Beth walked in with Mrs. Atwood trailing a few feet behind. They both smiled when they saw the children helping their old Papa in their Momma's absence. Anna Beth thanked each one of the kids individually, and then added, "Everyone, Grandma Laura is going to stay with us for a bit." My wife's gaze tangled with mine for just a second, and her forced smile clearly said, *What other choice do I have?* I nodded at her encouragingly. She had other choices, but I believed she was making the right one to hear her mother out. If I ever had the courage to talk to my other children again, I would at least hope they would give me a chance.

It was a quiet supper, however, with Michael and I carrying most of the conversation. We all distracted ourselves by watching Louisa's antics, which she ate up like pudding; she was the character of the family. After Anna Beth tucked the children into bed, bunking Joy in with Michael and settling her mother into Joy's room, she joined me in our bedroom. She looked utterly exhausted as she lowered herself onto the side of the bed, taking a deep breath and letting it out slowly.

I sat next to her for a few minutes, caressing her back supportively, and finally took her hand in mine as I spoke first. "What do you think, Angel?" She watched my thumb rub her knuckles and then gave my hand a gently squeeze.

"There used to be a time I thought if I could just *see* Momma again and know what happened, it would fix me, you know?" she replied, her voice quivering. "But it's like no matter how hard I try to fill this hole in my heart, it always opens back up and sinks more of my life into it."

I thought carefully of my own life lived with so many regrets and said softly, "Well, if it's any consolation, maybe her coming here isn't really about you at all... maybe *she's* the one that needs fixing."

17

Mrs. Atwood stayed with us for a week and a half. Neither Joy nor Michael was very happy about the sleeping arrangement, but they could both sense that this woman's visit was terribly important to their Momma and did not complain. In fact, Joy, with all her intuitiveness, tended to Michael and Louisa like *she* was their mother. It was a good thing, too. Anna Beth was quite distracted those long days and barely holding together with string.

Tensions ran high that first week especially; everyone was cordial enough when we were all together, but as soon as Anna Beth and her mother were away from the family, I could hear the whispered, edgy tones resume between the two of them. My wife hadn't told me what all was being said, not even in the privacy of our bedroom at night. I figured she was so tired from just living through it that by night she needed to digest and rest. By the weekend, the kids and I were itching to get out of the pressure-cooker, so I volunteered to take them fishing and swimming at our favorite pond down in the holler. I also hoped the time alone would give Anna Beth and her mother space to have it out properly, and we would come home to a more peaceful house.

When we came back that evening, however, Anna Beth fried up our prized catch of fish without a word while Mrs. Atwood stayed out on the porch. She only came in when Joy invited her to supper, going straight to her room afterwards. I figured the women would have to agree to disagree and part ways, neither of them truly satisfied, but was shocked to still find her there on Sunday morning, dressed and ready to accompany her daughter and grandchildren to church!

I held the farmhouse door open for them all to pass, welcoming the chance to stay home alone. Sitting on the front porch in solitude while smoking my pipe was the first time I felt my muscles relax since Mrs. Atwood's arrival. A couple hours later, when I saw my family break through the trees and into the clearing, I sighed, readying myself for another stressful afternoon. Then I noticed something was different. I stood from the rocker and squinted in the direction of the creek. The women were *smiling* as they walked toward the house, Anna Beth's arm linked in her mother's! I knew right then that I had missed something very important – the turning point in their relationship must have been reached. *But how?* I deliberated. For the life of me, I couldn't fathom how their wounds could have been healed in one afternoon after days of tension! As they came up on the porch, Anna Beth winked at me. She followed her mother inside to get lunch on while the kids ran to me with hugs and kisses.

I was further dumbfounded when the next couple of days smoothly passed by; they were even *enjoyable.* Not only were the kids comfortable with their Grandma Laura, but Anna Beth had started calling her Momma again. When it was time for Mrs. Atwood to leave – heading on to visit her youngest daughter in Tennessee – a mix of happy and sad tears were shed on both her and Anna Beth's part. I still wondered how they had managed to settle such an unfortunate past in one visit, but I was genuinely thankful they had – especially for Anna Beth's sake. She had waited a long time for that closure.

We drove Mrs. Atwood to the train station in the coup, and Anna Beth and the kids took turns hugging her good-bye. She asked if she could visit again, and I watched quietly as Anna Beth hugged her a second time, choking out the words, "Please do. You're welcome here any time, Momma." As soon as she boarded the train, I wrapped my arms tightly around my wife. The kids waved until the train disappeared over the horizon, its tall stacks belching black smoke into the air in great puffs. On the way home, Anna Beth held my hand in the car and just stared out her window as the kids talked quietly amongst themselves in the backseat. I hoped she would see her mother again, but like me and Elliott, a person just didn't know these things.

Later that afternoon, when the older kids were out playing in the yard and Louisa was down for a nap, Anna Beth finally opened up. We were resting on the porch, swaying gently back and forth on the swing while listening to the birds' chirps and titters from the trees.

"I *did* have it in me to forgive her again, even after hearing the rest of the story," Anna Beth confided quietly.

I smiled. "I'm glad you were able to reconcile, really I am... but I just don't see how you managed it," I admitted, shaking my head. She shrugged her shoulders with a sigh.

"I listened as she told me what happened after she and Daddy left us, and she listened as I told her everything that happened at the Graingers – *everything* – and we just kept trying to understand the reality the other lived through," she attempted to explain. "Momma apologized, of course. She wished she could take it all back and change what happened. She felt terribly guilty that Daddy died and none of us got to say goodbye... she even said she knew he was all us girls' favorite. She also admitted she was the one that pushed the move to Kentucky, and that splitting us up among the townsfolk was her idea, too. As upset as it all made me, I believe she earnestly thought it would be best. She was a tough mother, but she wouldn't have hurt us intentionally... not in a million years." Anna Beth grew quiet for a moment, collecting her thoughts. "I hope Daddy forgave her before he died. It was all just good dreams gone sour, I think."

I nodded, my mind still chewing on one more question. "Something happened last Sunday, though," I pressed. "You all came back from church, and everything seemed forgotten... like the two of you picked up where you left off when you were twelve."

Anna Beth's smile had a special glow about it, reminiscent of when I saw her get a blessing – as she called it – in church. I had accompanied her enough over the years to know that people, including her, sometimes got overwhelmed with emotion. They said it was God's spirit causing them to testify, sing, or shout about how good the Lord was. Their faith was something I still didn't understand, and I figured I was too old to try now anyway. However, the wonder of it pricked at me occasionally. Whatever Anna Beth had inside her, it made her believe in something beyond this world that somehow made life make sense. I desired that kind of conviction.

"God sent the gospel that Sunday, Mr. Johnston," Anna Beth continued gently. "It was exactly what Momma and I both needed. She got in the Spirit and testified about how she had made many mistakes in her life, but the one thing she did that she never regretted was finding the Lord." Anna Beth's smile lit up her tired face as she recalled the memory. "The part that God saved inside of me connected with the saved part inside of her, and I *felt* her testimony… that's how it is for all of God's people. When one reaches charity, the others feel it, too. God let me know right in my heart that it was time to forgive and let go of the past… that everything on earth is temporal and will pass away, but His Truth will stand forever. That's all that matters in this world."

I sat quietly for a long time, not meeting her eyes. I was somewhat ashamed when I finally admitted, "I don't really understand what you're talking about. If I had been a better person in life, maybe I would have found what you found somewhere along the way. I think it's too late for me now."

We both were aware the conversation had shifted and was no longer about her mother. Anna Beth tenderly intertwined her fingers in mine and squeezed. "Jesus died on the cross to save every honest heart, Mr. Johnston – man, woman, boy, girl, every race and color… it's never too late for any of us to seek God's mercy and grace when he can give us a broken and contrite spirit to do so," she replied quietly.

After several minutes of swinging in silence, she spoke again. "God also brought back to my memory how I was in the right place at the right time – with Mr. Jingle and Grace in Harlan – to get saved. He took my poor circumstances and made a way for me to find Him when I thought all was forsaken. It was the best gift I ever received, and it made every struggle in my life worthwhile."

I considered her beliefs carefully. Anna Beth often talked about how she *felt* God's Spirit, but I had always figured I was feeling the same thing – just through reverencing the Creator of nature on my walks. Now I wasn't so sure. Her faith seemed to run deeper and was more refined than my feelings. It honestly baffled me how she could say everything she suffered at the hand of Mr. Grainger was worth it to find this salvation. *How could she find such peace with her harrowing childhood – with the mother who caused it?* I wondered. The answers were inconceivable to me; I guess partly because at my core, I never believed *my* children could forgive *me* even if I tried to reconcile. I took a deep breath, trying to understand what she was saying. "How did what you suffered help you get saved?" I asked.

"Well, I think I have to tell you my experience of when the Lord saved my soul for you to really understand where I'm coming from," Anna Beth suggested. I nodded for her to continue as something squeezed inside my chest. She had talked about her salvation many times but never told me about it in detail. Perhaps that was what I needed to know to find it myself.

"I actually got saved the same night Mr. Grainger beat me," she began. "Mr. Jingle had stopped to talk to me along the road, and Mr. Grainger was furious. I'm sure he was worried people would figure out I was carrying his baby, not Chancey Durrett's, but Mr. Grainger kicked Mr. Jingle's cane out from under him and broke my arm dragging me back to the house. He was going to teach me a lesson about respect." Anna Beth paused, her jaw set tight with the memory. "When Grace ran out of the house to help me, he turned his rage on her. It was *bad*, Mr. Johnston. He was headed for Olivia, too, and Grace ran to help her... and I just ran. I hid in the church because I figured that was the last place he'd ever look for me." My wife glanced at me, and I wrapped my arm around her shoulders. It wasn't a particularly chilly night, but she was shaking.

"Go on, honey," I urged her. I genuinely desired to hear the experience that was not only the beginning of her faith but had the power to shine through our whole married lives.

"I was *so* broken," she whispered in a quivering voice. "I felt completely alone in the world, like the orphan I was... I just wept and wept. Then Mr. Jingle walked in. He hadn't been in a church since his family had died in that fire, but remember how I told you he was a preacher before he was a peddler? Well, God *sent* him to preach to *me*! He followed that feeling, found me in the church, and he preached exactly what my heart needed to hear that night. It was truly amazing." She started laughing, and I could see joy replacing the bitterness.

"I had this overwhelming feeling to bow at the altar and beg the Lord to save my soul, and at some point, Grace came in with Livie. She and Mr. Jingle prayed alongside me until I had begged all I could and didn't know what else to do, then I felt a still, small voice whisper, *Hug Grace.*"

"God *talked* to you?" I interrupted, skepticism creeping back into my thoughts.

Anna Beth nodded. "Not with words that you hear with your ears, like you and I are talking to each other, but God talks with a *feeling*. It's like..." she scrunched her face up, pondering how to describe it, "it's like I *thought* it, but my heart was pounding along with the thought, and I just knew hugging Grace was what the Lord wanted me to do! I didn't really *want* to hug Grace, though," she chuckled. "I was still mad at her for believing the town gossip about me! But, I *had* promised God I would do anything if He would just save my soul. So, the next time

I felt His urging, I made up my mind to reach for Grace. As soon as I opened my arms, the burden that had bowed me so low just rolled away, and I was free! I felt this calm, still, unshakeable peace. In that moment, I knew everything would be okay. It was like I had dug down deep and hit the rock. Nothing can move me off it now; I'm anchored in His love forevermore."

I didn't say a word. I didn't know what to say, so I just nodded. Her story was a lot to take in – it was so miraculous it didn't seem believable.

"So, anyway… back to Momma," Anna Beth said with a sigh. "The same charity God put in my heart when he saved me as a girl… that's what I felt last Sunday with Momma. She has salvation down deep in her soul, too. It's an eternal bond that nothing in this natural world, or what happened in the past, can mar – because it's *spiritual*. That is how I was able to fully forgive her for abandoning us, and probably the *only* reason I could. I wouldn't have been strong enough to show such grace in this flesh alone… but God strengthened me."

I patted her leg. "That's truly amazing," I mumbled, and I meant it. "I'm so happy that you have such a close connection with God."

My wife opened her mouth to say something else but thought better of it as the screen door squeaked open. We watched Louisa wander out, rubbing sleep from her eyes. Her golden-brown curls were all mussed up and sticking out like she had been shocked. It made Anna Beth and I both laugh, lightening the serious mood that had enveloped us.

"Did someone wake up?" Anna Beth smirked, holding her arms out to our youngest. Louisa drifted over to us, still woozy from her nap, and climbed into her Momma's lap.

"Where's Sissy and Bubby?" she asked with a yawn, looking around the yard.

"They're out playing somewhere," Anna Beth told her with a squeeze and kiss. I cleared my throat.

"How about we go find them?" I asked Louisa, seizing the opportunity to stretch my legs and meditate on the previous conversation away from my sweet, but perplexing wife.

The little girl nodded and slid out of her mother's lap, sucking on her finger while I struggled to my feet. Once I got the cane under me, I held my hand out to her. She slipped her little fist in mine, and I gave it a loving squeeze; it fit just perfectly. With a wink at my wife, we set off down the steps and toward the trees and stream – where always before lodged my sense of peace.

Part 3

Going Where I've Never Been

18

Touched deeply by the reconciliation between Anna Beth and her mother, I wrote Clara and each of our eight children an apology letter the next day. I did my best to explain why I left and who I had striven to become since then, and how, in the end, I hoped for their understanding and forgiveness. Anna Beth was overjoyed with my decision to reach out to my first family, and even more so when I started attending church with her and the kids every Sunday. After we had our deep heart-to-heart on the porch, it was a painful realization that what I had paled in comparison to what she had spiritually. If there was something more out there to find – besides just being the finest man I could be – I wanted to at least search for it. I knew it was a long shot, but I had an inkling that if I could just get a hold of it, *it* could fill the aching within me that not even Anna Beth's love could touch.

The members of the church were pleasantly surprised to see me, especially the Mutters. On the third week in a row, James invited me to sit up front with him. I chuckled and waved off the offer, telling him I preferred the back of the house as I just wanted to watch and listen – not participate or anything. Brother Ray was still the pastor, and, for a month or two, I tried my best to make sense of his sermons. He'd read from the Bible, come down from the stand and slowly walk around the altar until he really got going, then he'd be shouting and jumping about like someone lit a fire under him! I could see the congregation going with the feeling, like they were all making a journey through the service together, and how the fire caught from one to another in rapid succession – but I couldn't *feel* a thing. Anna Beth and I had a few more conversations about church in general – how men of God didn't plan out what to say yet preached by revelation – and she just begged me to keep coming. She was sure if I'd come, God would eventually reveal himself to me. It wasn't until Brother Ray stood up one Sunday morning solemnly saying, "There're lost among us, n'I want t'see 'em saved… search y'hearts. Is it you? Time's runnin' out, m'friend," that something changed for me in an instant.

The same tightness in my chest I had felt when Anna Beth told me her experience took hold and didn't let go. I listened intently as the preacher opened the Bible and read aloud, "*Enter y'in at the strait gate: fo' wide is the gate, n'broad is the way, that leadeth t'destruction, n'many there be which go in there at: 'cause strait is the gate, n'narrow is the way, which leadeth unto life, n'few there be that find it.*" He quietly flipped a few pages and read a few more verses. "*Then Peter said unto 'em, Repent, n'be baptized ev'ry one o'ya in the name o'Jesus Christ fo' the remission o'sins, n'ye shall receive the gift o'the Holy Ghost.*"

He closed the book, his hand resting on the cover in contemplation, and then came down from the stand. I watched him walk back and forth in the altar, part of me scared and part of me excited as he gathered his thoughts. The burning sensation magnified enough that I had to shift positions uncomfortably. I thought about leaving and never coming back, but when Anna Beth reached over and took my hand in hers, I resolved to wait this out one more time.

"We b'lieve that men're called b'God t'preach the Gospel, n'I've never been t'school t'*learn* how t'do this," the preacher spoke quietly at first, his voice gaining strength and volume. "We b'lieve that God can preach a man through revelation… so I don't know what I can say t'day from that scripture unless God gives me the words." He pulled a handkerchief out of his pocket and dabbed the gathering sweat from his brow.

Soon enough, Brother Ray's voice took on a different sound and rhythm all its own. I knew Anna Beth had told me so, but I realized for myself that he really *didn't* have anything planned out to say. *God* was instructing us through this man; he was just a mouthpiece. *If God could talk through him, couldn't he also talk to me?* I considered.

He went on to preach about how we all had an original sin on us because of Adam's fall in the Garden of Eden, and how Jesus was the only one found worthy to make a way to heaven… but that way was the narrow gate that few people found. "Why doesn't ev'ryone find it?" the preacher asked loudly. "'Cause *pride* keeps mankind from humble repentance, n'man can only b'truly saved when they realize they're at His mercy! They mus' come t'Him with a broken heart n'contrite spirit!"

The longer he preached, the more fear gripped me. I hadn't been that afraid of anything since I was a boy. *What am I so afraid of, though?* I questioned, trying to rationalize my growing anxiety. *God is supposed to be the embodiment of love…*

"Fear is the beginnin' o'wisdom; if t'day y'hear m'voice, harden not y'hearts!" Brother Ray said, his words answering my silent thoughts without missing a beat.

My heart started to pound in my chest. It was getting hot in that little church house. I worried I was having a heart attack, yet I sat still, completely captivated by this new spiritual awareness. *All my life I assumed death was it… but if there is a heaven to gain and hell to shun as this man preached, what if I stand before God in judgement and am found lacking?* My heart ached as I thought back on my life; there were a multitude of things that were probably considered sin. *God would never save a wretch like me,* I concluded miserably. *I don't stand a chance of finding His forgiveness and grace.*

"Y'may b'sittin' there thinkin': *Why would God save me?* 'Cause Jesus came t'save *ev'ry* honest person that b'lieves fully on Him! If y'want salvation more than anythin' else in this world, if y'truly desire t'b'reconciled with the One who created *ev'rythin'* – includin' *you* – y'can find it… n'it'll b'the greatest gift y'ever receive," the preacher was saying. He started to laugh, wiping tears from his eyes, and an older woman by the piano raised her hands, reared back, and shouted praises to God like she just couldn't contain the emotion anymore. The sound echoed around the church house and stirred that burning feeling in me to near boiling point. "But y'will have t'give up y'ways n'search it out with all y'heart; search it out fo' y'self like ev'ry las' one o'us," the preacher finished strong, a relieved smile lighting up his face. He made his way back to the stand, wiping his face dry with a handkerchief. He motioned toward the song leader. "The Lord said that's enough; get us a good song, brother, n'let's meet in the altar."

The choir started singing a resounding verse of *Amazing Grace* as everyone got to their feet. I watched people move toward each other with such heartfelt fellowship as they shook hands and hugged that it brought tears to my eyes. "Amazing Grace, how sweet the sound...," they sang. *How did the preacher know what I needed to hear?* I wondered. "That saved a wretch like me?" people continued to sing. *How did the choir know to sing the song that fit so perfectly with my feelings?* "I once was lost, but now am found; T'was blind but now I see!"

As if someone took blinders off an old horse, my eyes were fully opened to God's Truth. It had been simple enough for a child to understand all along! This *feeling way* my wife had lived in front of me for years was *real*. I had been privileged to encounter it for years, yet I nearly missed it altogether! I had been so focused on my mortal grief and happiness that I had failed to consider the most important thing of all: that we all have an immortal soul and will spend eternity somewhere. *Where am I going after I die?* I now contemplated the question with all my heart. The preacher had said time was running out, and for me that was certain! I could die before I made it back to our farmhouse.

The service continued to its end, but I didn't hear any other song or testimony. Anna Beth, who had gone to fellowship in the altar, was walking down the aisle toward me with concern etched in her face; I knew I must have been a sight. I didn't hardly know my right hand from my left. "Mr. Johnston are you okay?" she asked, reaching out to touch my arm. I remembered we were supposed to join the Mutters for lunch after church, but I felt sick thinking about it. I couldn't go and just pretend everything was fine when everything was all wrong. My chest felt like a bunch of rusty cogwheels grinding into motion. There was an urgency I needed to *move* with, or surely my body would just give out under the pressure.

I shuffled toward the door, mumbling, "I don't feel well – I'm going to walk on home, Honey. You and the kids go over to James and Rose's... I'll be fine."

Anna Beth nodded and stepped aside to let me pass, although I knew it went against every fiber of her being. I glanced back at her before pushing through the door and saw Rose patting her arm. They both were watching me with worried expressions. I felt guilty that I didn't have time to answer their questions; all I could think about was getting out of there! I wasn't even sure why. I just knew I needed to head home – something was a drawing me that way that I couldn't explain even if I tried.

I hurried as fast as I could with a cane to the hidden safety of the woods, following alongside the little stream that usually brought me such joy. I thought I'd feel better once I was away from the church and those people, but the heaviness in my heart only expanded. It was like a suffocating weight I was struggling to move against. I wanted it off me but was helpless to move it. That's when I began to weep, wiping at my tears with the sleeve of my shirt as I pushed myself forward. *What in the world is wrong with me?* I pondered. *Is this the same feeling Anna Beth talks about? Is this God?* As soon as I considered the possibility, I felt the whispering voice of hope: *I am.* Gusts of wind sent leaves spiraling across my path, leaving me breathless. I was near an old tree stump and almost to our house when I couldn't go another step. I fell on my knees, bowed my head, and grabbed onto that old tree stump for dear life.

"What do you want from me?" I cried out loud, believing the God who gave me this heavy burden could hear me wherever I was. I thought I had been a strong and good enough man most my life, but I was finally seeing myself as is – an unworthy wretch who had honored the *creation* more than the *Creator.* I had no idea how to pray like the people of Still Valley, but there was a groaning working within me that I just began to talk through. I said whatever words came to me, mostly begging the Lord to forgive me of my foolish, sinful ways, for all the things I didn't know, and to save me so I could go to heaven with Anna Beth. The thought of being separated from her for all eternity turned my tears to the bitterest weeping. "I'll do anything. Take my life if you must – just save my soul first!" I cried.

Right then, this gentle breeze blew through my soul, lifting my burden and leaving in its wake this incredible sense of calm. *Is this it? Is this how it feels to be saved?* I wondered in blessed relief. I lifted my head toward heaven, still gripping that old stump, and laughed, knowing the answer was *yes.* It was a new sound in my ears, like it was coming from a different man! Now I understood that old gospel song they sang sometimes, *Peace Like a River...* salvation was like a cool drink of water drawn from a deep well when I had been thirsty to the point of death. It felt so good I thought I could live for another hundred years and never tire of the feeling!

I don't know how long I knelt there laughing and thanking the Lord for the change He made in me... but when I finally came to myself, Anna Beth was running toward me. The leaves crunched under her feet as I stood up, my cane still leaning against the stump.

"Mr. Johnston!" she cried. "There you are... I've been *so* worried!"

She ran into my open arms and hugged my waist tightly. "James and Rose brought us home, and when you weren't there…"

"Anna Beth," I said softly, stroking her hair. She looked up at me, tears in her eyes. "Anna Beth, God *saved* me… right here by this old stump. I've set my sails toward home, and I know I'll make it alright." That joyful laugh erupted from me again as my new hope bubbled back up in an instant. My wife covered her mouth and shouted – it was a beautiful sound, like she was ringing the bells of heaven with her voice. As our hearts collectively overflowed with joy, the peace I had felt when the burden rolled away came breezing back by my heart. I put my hands on her face in amazement. "I didn't just hear that shout; I *felt* it!" I exclaimed, amazed to finally understand how the Spirit of God could connect people together.

We both cried happy tears as Anna Beth hugged me again. "I *knew* something good was going to happen today!" my wife confessed. "The Lord told me! We've all been praying for you for such a long time, Mr. Johnston."

I pulled her close to my chest with so much love I felt my heart would burst. "You're the best thing the Lord ever gave me… *next* to my salvation," I replied with a wink. She laughed again, shaking her head. "I understand what you were talking about now, how you could forgive your mother and put your past behind you once and for all because letting go of the natural kept you close to the spiritual – to this wonderful feeling." I looked around the woods; the radiant light was shining through the branches and shimmering on the leaves. "I feel like God moved everything around in my whole life to bring me to this very time and place."

"Salvation is worth it all," she said contentedly. "It's really the only thing that matters."

I took my wife's warm hand in my palm, and, together, we walked home. James and Rose Mutter were sitting on the front porch with the children, and when they saw us, everyone jumped up and hurried to meet us halfway.

"Mr. Johnston! We were so upset when y'weren't home yet," Rose spoke first. Joy hugged her mother while Louisa wrapped her arms around my leg.

"Yeah, Papa, why did it take you so long to get here?" Michael asked, shoving his hands deep into his pockets.

I grinned at all of them and held my hand out to James. "Shake hands with a new man," I said. My friend's face lit up with instant recognition, and Rose and Anna Beth *both* started shouting praises to the Lord. James laughed and tears came to his eyes as he firmly shook my hand, pulling me into a tight hug. That gentle breeze blew through my heart again, stirring up that new, unrivaled love inside, and I knew we had all things common. We each had our own experience, but it *felt* the same!

When everyone settled down, the kids ran off to play while Anna Beth and I sat on the porch with our friends. I told them the whole story, how I had wanted to know more about the *Old-Time Way*, as they called it, for a very long time. I also told them how the preaching scared me that morning and a burden fell on me so heavy I had to pray it off with God's help in the woods.

"Fear is the beginnin' o'wisdom, n'no one can get saved without fear n'the God-given conviction that works a repentance unto life ev'rlasting," James interjected.

"Well, I guess repenting is what I did by that old stump!" I chuckled. "It was like I poured myself out to God and just *felt* better. The burden rolled away, and I'm completely at peace. That's the only way I can describe it."

James was nodding in understanding. "That's what salvation is, my friend. It's blessed assurance, a covenant with God himself. You met his conditions, and He gave you a great gift... it's near indescribable, isn't it?"

I took a deep breath and let it out slowly. I had smiled so much my cheeks were beginning to hurt. The Mutters stayed and talked the day away, Anna Beth and Rose eventually disappearing inside to fix supper for us all. Alone on the porch, I thanked James for praying for me, when I didn't even know I needed to be prayed for, and he just patted my arm with a grin on his face. I had thought marrying Anna Beth was the happiest day of my life, but this day topped even that! God had been *so* good to me, and I hadn't deserved not one ounce of it. Through His mercy, He really *did* save an old wretch like me. *Amazing* didn't tell the half of it. It was truly better felt than told.

19

I was going to join Still Valley and be baptized, but I never got the chance. None of us knew how close my time was… none of us, but the Creator Himself. I fell ill shortly after my experience in the woods, and the doctor said he already heard the beginning of pneumonia in my lungs. Anna Beth did her best to nurse me back to health a second time, but it was, at last, my time to shed those bars of bone.

James and Rose brought the kids by to see me every day. Joy Elizabeth and Michael Anthony cried, but I told them not to worry, that everything was going to be okay, and I loved them more than life itself. Little Louisa, who recently turned three, was just getting big enough to climb up on the bed next to me all by herself. "Papa?" she said innocently. "When you gonna get up again?"

I smiled and held my hand out to her, and she nuzzled her cheek into my palm with a smile of her own. She might have had Anna Beth's hair and grit, but she had my smile and mischievousness. "Honey, I'm just sailing up and around the bend where you can't see me, but one day you'll catch up. We'll all go into heaven *together*, okay? I'll wait for you at the gate," I promised. She nodded her head, those curls bobbing around, and gave me a quick kiss before running off to play with her sister.

When my health deteriorated enough that I was barely clinging to consciousness, Rose took the children to her house to stay while Anna Beth sat at my bedside around the clock. One of the days I stirred awake, with just a little bit of strength left, I found my wife holding my hand. She had been watching me sleep.

"A letter came for you," she said softly. "It's from Elliott."

I laughed in disbelief, which sent me straight into a coughing spell. I hacked until I gagged, finally stopping only to gasp for breath and press my head back to the pillow. I hated for her to see me so overcome with frailty, but at the same time I was thankful for her enduring presence. She helped me roll over and firmly patted my back, then rubbed her hand in circles to try and move the fluid and mucous from my lungs. When I finally caught my breath, she gently laid me back down and held my hands.

"Read it to me, please," I whispered. I was beyond grateful my friend was still alive and that I got to hear from him one last time. Anna Beth opened the letter and cleared her throat.

Dear Daniel, she read.

Hey, old buddy. I'm sorry I haven't written in so long. I appreciated all your letters during my recovery. It's been a rough road with one trouble after another, but I'll spare you the grizzly details. I've thought about more important things I wanted to tell you so many times... but I don't know if I can even put it all into words. I'll try.

When I got to visit you and your beautiful family, we talked for a long time on the front porch. I'm sure you remember. I was worried about my life not meaning anything to anybody... that I had missed the goal of life. But this letter isn't about me. I want you to know I am genuinely happy that you found joy with that sweet little lady of yours. Your life matters to her and those sweet kids of yours, and your life has mattered to me; your friendship has been a constant through the years. The love you and Anna Beth share, fifty years apart – some people would say it was impossible, that it's nothing more than a marriage of money and convenience. But I've watched you all together, and you truly found love, my friend! You've been courageous enough to live it out in front of so many critics. Tell your story, Daniel. The world deserves to know what is possible... even for old soldiers like us.

I hope this letter finds you well and that one day we may meet again.

Sincerely,
Elliott

Anna Beth had tears in her eyes when she handed it to me so I could see my friend's words, and I held it a long time in my shaking hands. I had thought back on that conversation of Elliott's and mine so many times as well.

"I told him, that day on the porch, that if you found joy and happiness in life – with people, the things you did, or whatever – that you've reached the goal," I recalled solemnly, barely able to speak. I looked at my wife with a sense of urgency flooding my exhausted body. "Anna Beth, you must tell him that I found an even higher calling than joy in this world. Please, will you make sure to tell him that what is natural is going to pass away like our old bodies, but what the Lord gives us will be eternal?" I turned my palm up with great effort and reached my hand out to her. She wiped a tear from her cheek and encased her hands around mine. "I need to know you'll tell him for me...."

My wife nodded. "I'll do my best to tell him what matters," she promised.

"And you raise our children in church. Make sure they have the opportunity to be saved," I rasped, feeling weaker by the minute. "I want to see them when I wake up in glory, but more than that, I want them to know their Heavenly Father loves them more than I ever could. He'll take care of them when I'm gone, like He has taken care of you since your Daddy left."

More tears came to Anna Beth's eyes, and she sobbed as my breathing shallowed. It was like I was sucking air through a straw and not getting enough. I knew the death angels were close, yet I wasn't scared of what was to come. I could still feel the peace I had first felt when I knelt by that old stump; it settled around my body like a warm, heavy blanket. My body didn't even hurt anymore.

Anna Beth put her hand on my cheek, and I tried to turn my face to kiss her fingers. She leaned over and gently kissed my forehead instead. My strength was trickling away, my body seemingly sinking into the bed. I kept my eyes on her, though, wanting her face to be the last thing I saw this side of heaven. She was *so* beautiful, my angel from the post office.

"I love you, Mr. Johnston," she whispered. Her strength was still a marvel; she didn't lower her eyes to the grief. "You taught me what true love is... gentle, kind, *unconditional*."

A light shining in the distance captured my attention, and I just knew deep down that everything was going to be alright. I wanted her to understand I could see it all clearly now – even though they'd inevitably have troubles and trials, God was going to continue to take care of her and our kids in my absence. I took a deep, rattling breath. My words came out raspy and sounded far away to me. "You're going to be okay, my love," I managed to say. "You tell our story so other people know. Tell the whole world how age didn't matter, and... and I'll see you on the other side."

Anna Beth nodded, leaning forward with another sob. She smiled through her tears, rubbing my cheek gently with her thumb. I barely felt the movement, but her hand was wonderfully warm. "I'm *so* thankful God gave me you," she replied.

I gave a little nod. "God knew exactly what He was doing when He put us together, Angel. You were not only my joy, but you were my way to Him."

She kissed me again, and the edges of my vision grew brighter. I kept my eyes on Anna Beth, my angel, and forgot about my struggle to breathe. I forgot about moving my heavy muscles, too; I just relaxed into the gentle breeze that was filling every part of my being. A whole camp of angels had slipped their hands under me and was lifting my spirit upward. The image of my wife faded as I closed my eyes, and my sight filled with brilliant light. *Glory, glory – this is what living was all about...*

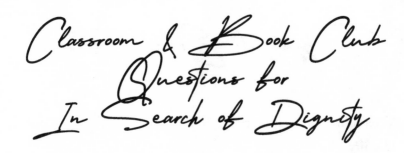

Classroom & Book Club Questions for In Search of Dignity

- ❖ The story begins with this sentence: *The war that nearly tore this world apart tore me apart instead.* In what ways do we learn Daniel has been torn apart? Discuss the physical, mental, and emotional difficulties veterans face when assimilating back into civilian life.

- ❖ In any conflict, the adage "There are two sides to every story" rings true. What blame is to be placed on Daniel versus Clara, and what unfortunate circumstances were outside of their control?

- ❖ Discuss Daniel's "wandering years" and how he squandered his second chance at life and happiness. What was he running from? Why couldn't he put down roots?

- ❖ When Daniel meets Anna Beth in the post office, it is love at first sight. Have you ever had an experience when you just *knew* something was right (even if others thought it was unconventional, like Daniel & Anna Beth's age difference)?

- ❖ Daniel and Anna Beth both have suffered from painful memories and are trying to move on. Discuss the possibility of how two "damaged" people can help each other, and therefore help themselves heal.

- ❖ Being abandoned herself, Anna Beth understands Daniel's children from his first marriage in a way he does not. Discuss how and why she gently encourages him to reconnect with them.

- ❖ Anna Beth's reunions with her sisters and, later, her mother have a profound effect on Daniel. What does Laura Atwood's visit and her reconciliation with Anna Beth finally spur him to do?

- ❖ The spiritual themes of forgiveness and redemption run throughout the book for several characters. Discuss how these themes come to full maturation for Daniel, Anna Beth, and her mother, Laura Atwood.

- ❖ In the end, Daniel can look back and see how God mercifully directed his pathways to get him to a time and place where he could have the opportunity for salvation. Do you believe God can direct a person's footsteps in life even when they are unaware of it or feel as if they don't deserve his mercy and charity?

Suggested Essay Themes

- ❖ Veteran mental health/trauma/PTSD
- ❖ Dignity
- ❖ Divine leadership
- ❖ Family
- ❖ Personal growth
- ❖ Effects of loss
- ❖ Forgiveness
- ❖ Reconciliation/redemption
- ❖ Love
- ❖ Friendship

Q & A with the author

How did you come up with this story, and why did you tell it to the world?

In Search of Dignity is the third Christian historical fiction novel in my Dignity series, based on the story of my great-grandfather, John Daniel Elliott. My grandmother, Lois Elliott Duvall, told me everything she could remember about our ancestors, and his story before and after meeting my great-grandmother, May Wood Elliott Kerr, was one you just don't forget (even though parts of it were most likely embellished as he was known to be quite a character and talebearer!). As soon as I finished *When Dignity Came to Harlan* and *Teaching Dignity*, I knew I had to finish Anna Beth's story with Daniel's; it was the only way to do their legacy justice. I tell people all the time – truth is often stranger than fiction!

If your book is based on a true story, which parts of it are truth versus fiction?

My grandmother sat down with me one day in her little kitchen and told me everything she remembered about her father's life. She was only three when he passed, however, so luckily, we had other family members like a cousin, Annie Utick, descended from John Daniel Elliott's brother's family that had done extensive family research. Here are how the facts compare to the fiction within *In Search of Dignity*:

Did you do any research for your story?

Besides recording my grandmother's recollections and reading the detailed genealogy research from my cousin, I researched Harlan, Kentucky to get an idea of the landscape for the setting along with the rough 1920s to 1940s time period. The dates barely overlap (my ancestors, John and May, married in 1920 and he passed in 1932, while fictional characters, Daniel and Anna Beth, married in 1930 and he passed around 1943), so I had to research period details like travel, places/

events Daniel's wanderings could have taken him after the divorce, when electric lights/appliances and indoor plumbing came into the homes, the phonograph and Victrola, and what Lee's Catalogue was! My close friend and avid encourager of the Dignity series, Reverend Stephen Doyle, is always a wealth of information in this department as well – I originally had a Ferris wheel on Sanibel Island, and with his suggestion, changed it to a light house. That became one of my favorite scenes in the story!

Does the story end here?

In Search of Dignity is one half of my great-grandparents amazing story. While it *could* end here, it did not begin here! Anna Beth Atwood was once a child who overcame insurmountable odds to grow up and find joy in life... but to hear the beginning of the whole story, how the angel in the post office came to be, you must read it in her own words in *When Dignity Came to Harlan* and its sequel, *Teaching Dignity*. Will there be a book 4? Perhaps!

Truth

- John D. Elliott was born in 1845 in Boone County, Iowa, and fought in the Civil War for the Union. He was discharged for an injury that caused him to lose his eye (which was replaced with a glass one) and drew $100 in pension. He may have also sustained a closed-head brain injury when drug several feet behind a wagon, and he was committed to mental institutions at least twice within his life.

- John married Julia A. Endfield in 1867 and from that union came eight children: Charles M. "Charlie" (1868), Eldora Artemesia "Dora" (1870), John Jeremiah (1872), George Justin (1875), Walter Andrew (1877), Isa Dora (1879), Elmer William (1881), and Emma Alice (1883). They lived on 120 acres of land in Washington County, Idaho, and every month John would travel to check the perimeters. He claimed that one day he started on the trip but decided to come back early, finding his wife with the farm's foreman (or neighbor). However, John was known to tell tales, and these allegations were never proven in court. Julia was actually the first to file for divorce in 1904, but the case was dropped, most likely due to not being able to afford a lawyer. Two years after her filing, John filed for divorce citing desertion, not infidelity.

- John stayed in Idaho and married his second wife, Cynthia Carter, in 1908, but divorced her after a lengthy separation. He claimed he traveled the country for many years, saying, "I've seen every state in the union and have had a residence in half of them." In 1920, he married May Wood Elliott Kerr (who he had met in the post office) in Edmonson County, Kentucky (seven days after officially divorcing Cynthia). He was 73 years old and she only 24 (about 50 years apart)!

Fiction

- Daniel Johnston, a wealthy farm owner, leaves his home and wife in Oregon to fight a war. After the war, he suffers from the trauma he had witnessed as well as trying to blend back into civilian and family life – evident through his implied rough behavior, drinking, and stays in a mental institution.

- Daniel comes home to his wife, Clara, and his eight children (same names) after the war. She had kept the farm going in his absence, with the help of the foreman and farmhands. She had formed an unlikely bond with the foreman, George Walter, and took comfort in their affair – even after Daniel comes home. He is a changed man and not always kind to her even though he tries. When Daniel catches his wife and foreman together in the barn, he leaves his family and heads east to start another life on his own.

- Daniel travels the country for ten years and is now 75 years old. He stops to rest in Harlan County, Kenutcky, on his way to the Gulf, and meets Anna Beth Atwood in the post office. She had a troubled childhood but has overcome her obstacles as best she could. He falls in love with her at first sight. She is 25 years old – but 50 years apart in age doesn't matter to them.

Truth

- John bought May a house with two rooms and a porch across the front, a car, radio, phonograph, and beautiful dishes from Lee's Catalogue... all the finest things. She called him "Mr. Elliott" out of respect. From their union came three children: Joy Bell, Eddie, and Lois. They were the best dressed kids in the neighborhood, but they had chores and weren't spoiled. The children even had to go down to the creek and bring sandstone up to the house in a wagon so they could scrub the bacon grease that popped out of the skillet and stained the floors!

- May lost track of her parents and sisters in foster care as a child, but she reconnected with all of them – Betty, Clarcie, Maggie, and Cora. Betty stayed in Missouri, where their family originated, and Clarcie, who had run away from her foster home, made it back to her oldest sister! Maggie and Cora married, the latter marrying the son of her foster family. May's mother (who had visited her once in foster care to tell her their father had died) came for another visit when she was married, staying for a week or two.

- May was saved at 12 years old at Good Springs United Baptist Church and professed a strong faith in Christ all her life. John D. Elliott, who had roots in the Quaker religion, said he was of the Christian Scientist faith. However, on his death bed he patted May's hand and told her to raise the children in her religion. He was buried in a family graveyard on a farm whose land eventually became part of the Mammoth Cave National Park.

- John and May's youngest child, my grandmother, Lois Elliott Duvall, had only one memory of her father. They were walking in the yard together under some trees while she held onto his finger. She was only three years old when he passed.

- After John's death, May married Lewis Kerr and had three more children: Evelyn, Lewis Jr., and Bobby, all of whom were raised in church. May is buried in the graveyard at Fairview United Baptist Church in Edmonson County, Kentucky.

Fiction

- Daniel builds Anna Beth a new house on the outskirts of town with the best money had to offer: indoor plumbing, electric lights, a radio, phonograph, Victrola, and beautiful dishes and carnival glass from the Lee's Catalogue. Anna Beth calls him "Mr. Johnston" out of respect. They have three children together: Joy Elizabeth, Michael Anthony, and Louisa Rose are well-raised and mannerly children.

- Anna Beth had lost track of her parents and sisters in foster care, but she reconnects with all of them at the wedding – Martha, Janie, Emily, and of course Olivia (who lived with her, Grace, and Mr. Jingle). Martha had stayed in Missouri, where their family originated, and Janie, who had ran away from her foster home, made it all the way back to her older sister! Emily married the son of her foster family, and Olivia, also raised by Grace, was following in Anna Beth's footsteps with the plan to continue her education at Wesleyan College in Georgia. After Anna Beth is married, her mother finally makes contact and comes for a visit. That is when Anna Beth learned of her father's death and her mother's decision to leave them all in foster care for their own good.

- Anna Beth had been saved in July of 1920 as a 14 years old at the little church on the hill in Harlan County, Kentucky. She professed a strong faith in Christ all her life, and after telling Daniel (who had considered himself a Christian Scientist) her experience, he seeks the Lord. He finds salvation right before his death and tells her on his deathbed to raise the children in her faith – and to tell their story.

- Daniel and Anna Beth's youngest, Louisa Rose, is only three when he passed. Shortly before he falls ill, they take a walk together under the trees while she holds onto his finger.

- Anna Beth is with Daniel as he passes, and while we do not know what happens after – we know God will provide.

Acknowledgments

*How do I begin to thank the people who have encouraged me to
continue writing (and helped shape) the Dignity series?*

My deepest gratitude…

To my family, friends, and Dignity Fans for loving my Christian
historical fiction and encouraging me to write more in the series. When
a group of people helps you realize and makes a dream become reality,
they forever have cemented a place in your heart!

To my excellent Editorial Board members who not only caught
grammatical errors but helped me shape the story to be deeper and more
encompassing than I could ever imagine alone.

To Julie Werner and the team at Barefoot Publishing who has
immense faith in my writing and worked hard to bring *Dignity* to readers
all over the world.

Keep in Touch

Rebecca Duvall Scott
www.facebook.com/groups/whendignitycametoharlan
www.RebeccaDuvallScott.com
Rebecca@RebeccaDuvallScott.com